"When I Take You To My Bed This Time, It Will Be Far Better Than Ever Before."

"I will never sign an agreement to that!"

"And I'd never ask you to. This has nothing to do with the marriage deal. I'm only letting you know I want you in my bed. And you will come. Because you want to. Because you want me."

Her pupils fluctuated, her cheeks flushed. Proof positive of his claims.

Still she scoffed. "You really have to see someone for that head of yours, before it snaps off your neck under its own weight."

He buried his face in her neck, inhaled her, absorbing her shudder into his. "I don't want you in my bed. I need you there. I've craved you there for six long years."

Dear Reader,

Temporarily His Princess was such a treat to write! It was a much anticipated return to an exotic world I created years ago: my Mediterranean kingdom of Castaldini with its rich history and glamorous present. I revisited some of my most beloved characters, to get a delightful glimpse into their happily-ever-after. All that, while going along for the intensely passionate ride of two new star-crossed lovers as they navigate a turbulent journey to their own happiness, among so many obstacles, secrets and twists.

I loved writing Vincenzo and Glory's story as they overcome so much heartache, tear down so many barriers, inside and out, and come together in a much-deserved and glorious destiny. I really hope you enjoy reading their story as much as I did writing it!

I love to hear from readers, so please visit my website for my latest news at www.oliviagates.com, email me at oliviagates@gmail.com, and connect with me on Facebook, Goodreads and Twitter.

Thanks for reading!

Olivia Gates

OLIVIA GATES

TEMPORARILY HIS PRINCESS

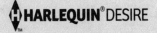

HARLEQUIN® DESIRE

Recycling programs
for this product may
not exist in your area.

ISBN-13: 978-0-373-73244-9

TEMPORARILY HIS PRINCESS

Copyright © 2013 by Olivia Gates

Printed in U.S.A.

TM www.Harlequin.com

Books by Olivia Gates

Harlequin Desire

   The Sarantos Secret Baby #2080
**To Touch a Sheikh* #2103
   A Secret Birthright #2136
††*The Sheikh's Redemption* #2165
††*The Sheikh's Claim* #2183
††*The Sheikh's Destiny* #2201
§*Temporarily His Princess* #2231

Silhouette Desire

 The Desert Lord's Baby #1872
The Desert Lord's Bride #1884
The Desert King #1896
†*The Once and Future Prince* #1942
†*The Prodigal Prince's Seduction* #1948
†*The Illegitimate King* #1954
  Billionaire, M.D. #2005
  In Too Deep #2025
    "The Sheikh's Bargained Bride"
**To Tame a Sheikh* #2050
**To Tempt a Sheikh* #2069

*Throne of Judar
†The Castaldini Crown
**Pride of Zohayd
††Desert Knights
§Married by Royal Decree

Other titles by this author
available in ebook format.

OLIVIA GATES

has always pursued creative passions such as singing and handicrafts. She still does, but only one of her passions grew gratifying enough, consuming enough, to become an ongoing career—writing.

She is most fulfilled when she is creating worlds and conflicts for her characters, then exploring and untangling them bit by bit, sharing her protagonists' every heart-wrenching heartache and hope, their every heart-pounding doubt and trial, until she leads them to an indisputably earned and gloriously satisfying happy ending.

When she's not writing, she is a doctor, a wife to her own alpha male and a mother to one brilliant girl and one demanding Angora cat. Visit Olivia at www.oliviagates.com.

To everyone at Harlequin, RWA, *RT Book Reviews,* NINC and *CataRomance* who helped me realize a dream and get to a much better place. No thanks are enough.

Prologue

Vincenzo froze as he heard someone fumbling open the door.
She was here.

Every muscle turned to rock, every nerve fired like a high-voltage cable. Then the door slammed with an urgent thud and frantic footsteps followed, each jarring his equilibrium with the force of an earthquake.

There'd been no alert from his guards. No doorbell had announced her arrival. She was the only one he'd ever given unlimited access and keys to his penthouse.

But he'd given her more than access to his personal space—he'd given her dominion over his priorities and passions. She'd been the only woman he'd fully trusted, believed in. Loved.

And it had all been a lie.

The spear embedded in his gut twisted. Rage. Mostly at himself.

Even after he'd gotten proof of her betrayal, he'd clung to the belief that it would be explained away. She'd had him that deeply in her power.

That alone should have alerted him something was seriously wrong. It wasn't in his nature to trust. He'd never let anyone come that close or become anywhere near that vital. As a prince of Castaldini, he'd always been suspicious of people's intentions. After he'd become *the* rising-star researcher in the cutthroat field of energy alternatives, he'd believed any hope of a genuine relationship was over.

Until her. Until Glory.

From the first glance, he'd reeled at the attraction that had kept intensifying. From the first conversation, he'd sunk into a well of affinity, the deepest he'd ever known. It had been magical, how they'd hungered, connected. She'd aroused his every emotion, appeased his every need—physical, intellectual and spiritual.

But he'd just been a means to an end. An end she'd achieved.

After the first firestorm of agony had almost wrecked him, logic had doused it with its sobering ice. Seeking retribution would have only compounded the damage. He'd decided to let pain consume him, rather than give her more than what she'd already snatched from him. He'd walked away without a word.

Not that she'd let him walk away.

Her nonstop messages had morphed from worried to frantic. With each one, his heart had almost exploded, first with the need to soothe her, then with fury at falling for her act yet again. Then had come that last message. A heart-stopping simulation of a woman going out of her mind fearing for her loved one's safety.

The pain had been so acute it had seared him with clarity.

He'd realized there could only be one reason behind her desperate persistence. Her plan must not be concluded yet. Even if she thought his avoidance meant he suspected her, she seemed to be willing to risk anything to get close to him again, to pull the strings of his addiction to her for the opportunity to finish what she started.

So he'd let her find out he'd returned. He'd known she'd zoom right over to corner him.

But though he'd planned this face-off, he wasn't ready. Not for the sight of her, or for what he had to do.

Mannaggia! He shouldn't have given her the chance to invade his life again for any reason. He just wasn't *ready....*

"*Vincenzo!*"

A pale creature, who barely resembled the vibrant one who'd captured him body and heart, burst into his bedroom.

She stumbled to a halt, eyes turbid and swollen with what so convincingly looked like incessant weeping, and stood facing him across the bedroom where they'd shared unimaginable pleasures for the past six months.

Before another synapse could fire, she exploded across the room. Before he could draw another breath, her arms were around him, clinging like a woman would to a life raft.

And he knew. He'd missed it all, every nuance of her. He'd yearn for her, the woman he'd loved but who didn't exist, until the end of his days.

His mind unraveled with the need to crush her back, breathe her in so he could breathe again. He struggled not to bury his aching hands in her hair, not to drag her face to his and take of her breath. His lips went numb, needing to feel hers, just one last time....

As if sensing his impending capitulation, she surged up, pulled his head down and stormed his face in kisses.

Temptation tightened around his throat like a noose. His hands moved without volition.

They stopped before they closed around her, his body going rigid as if guarding against a blow as what she'd been reiterating in that tremulous, strangled voice sank into his fogged awareness.

"My love, my love."

Barely suppressing a roar, he clamped her arms before she sucked him dry of will and coherence.

She reluctantly let him separate them, raised the face that had embodied his desires and hopes. Her heavenly eyes were drowning in those masterfully feigned emotions.

"Oh, darling, you're all right." She hugged him again, seamlessly changing from overwrought relief to agitated curiosity. "I went insane when you answered none of my calls. I thought something…terrible must have happened."

So that was her strategy. To play innocent to the last.

"Nothing happened."

Was that his voice? That inhuman rasp?

Pretending not to notice the ice that encased him, dread entered the eyes that hid her soullessness behind that facade of guilelessness. "Did you have another breach? Did your security isolate you this time until they could identify the leak?"

Was she that audacious? Or did she believe she was too ingenious to be exposed? If she *were* still secure in his obliviousness, she wouldn't conceive of any other reason he'd stay away while his security team investigated how his research results kept being leaked in spite of their measures.

Good. He preferred to play it that way. It gave him the perfect opportunity to play the misdirection card.

"There haven't been any breaches." He pretended a calm that had to be his greatest acting effort. "Ever."

Momentary relief was chased away with deepening confusion. "But you told me…" She stopped, at a loss for real this time.

Si, that was a genuine reaction at last. For he *had* told her—every detail of the incidents and the upheavals he'd suffered as his life's work was being systematically stolen. And she'd pretended such anguish at his losses, at her help-lessness to help him.

"Nothing I told you was true. I let decoy results get leaked. I had great pleasure imagining the spies' reactions when they realized *that,* not to mention imagining their punishment for delivering useless info. No one knows where or what my real results are. They're safe until I'm ready to disclose them."

Every word was a lie. But he hoped she'd relay those lies to her recruiters, hopefully making them discard it without testing it and finding out it *was* the real deal.

That chameleon hid her shock, seamlessly performing un-certainty with hurt hovering at its edges. "That's fantastic… but…why didn't you tell *me* that? You thought you were being monitored? Even…here?" She hugged herself, as if to ward off invasive eyes. "But a simple note would have saved me end-less anguish, and I would have acted my part for the spies."

He gritted his teeth. "Everyone got the version I needed them to believe, so my opponents would believe it along with them. Only my most trusted people got the truth."

She stilled. As if afraid to let his words sink in. "And I'm not among those?"

Searing relief scalded through him, that she'd finally given him the opening to vent some antipathy. "How could you be? You were supposed to be a brief liaison, but you were too clingy and I had no time for the hassle of terminating things with you. Not before I found an as-convenient replacement, anyway."

If he could believe anything from her anymore, he would have thought his words had stabbed her through the heart.

"R-replacement…?"

His lips twisted. "With my schedule, I can only afford sexual partners who jump at my commands. That's why you were so convenient, being so…compliant. But such accommodating lovers are hard to come by. I let one go when I find another. As I have."

Hurt blossomed in her eyes like ink through turquoise waters. "It wasn't like that between us…"

"What did you think it was? Some grand love affair? Whatever gave you that impression?"

Her lips shook, her voice now a choking tremolo. "You did… You said you loved me…."

"I loved your…performance. You did learn to please me exceptionally well. But even such a…malleable sex partner only…keeps up my interest for a short while."

"Was that all I am…was…to you? A sex partner?"

His heart quivered with the effort to superimpose the truth over her overwhelming act. "No. You're right. A partner indicates a somewhat significant liaison. Ours certainly wasn't that. Don't tell me that wasn't clear from day one."

He could have sworn his words hacked her like a dull blade. If he didn't have proof of her perfidy, the agony she simulated would have torn down his defenses. Its perfection only numbed him now, turning his heart to stone.

He wanted her to rant and rave and shed fake tears, giving him the pretext to tear harder into her. She only stared at him, tears a precarious ripple in her eclipsed eyes.

Then she whispered, "If—if this is a joke, please, stop…"

"Whoa. Did you actually believe you were more to me than a convenient lay?"

She jerked as if he'd backhanded her. His trembling hold on restraint slipped another notch. He had to get this over with before *he* started to rant, exposing the truth.

"I should have known you wouldn't take the abundant hints. From the way you believed my every word it was clear you lack any astuteness. You sure didn't become my executive projects manager through merit. But you're starting to anger me, acting as if I owe you anything. I already paid for your time and services with far more than either was worth."

Her tears finally overflowed.

They streaked her hectic cheeks in pale tracks, melting the last of his sanity, making him snarl, "Next time a man walks away, let him. If you'd rather not hear the truth about how worthless you were to him…."

"Stop…please…" Her hands rose, as if to block blows. "I know what I felt from you…it was real and intense. If—if you no longer feel this way, just leave me my memories…."

"Is that obliviousness or just obnoxiousness? Seems you've forgotten who I am, and don't know the caliber of women I'm used to. But it's not too late to give you a reality check. Your replacement is arriving in minutes. Care to hang around and get a sobering, humbling look at her?"

Her disbelief finally disintegrated and resignation seeped in to fill the vacuum it left behind.

She was giving up the act. At last. It was over.

He turned away, feeling like he'd just kicked down the last pillar in his world.

But she wouldn't let it be over, her tear-soaked words lodging in his back like knives. "I…loved you, Vincenzo. I *believed* in you…thought you an exceptional human being. Turns out you're just a sleazy user. And no one will ever know, since you're also a flawless liar. I wish I'd never seen you…hope one of my 'replacements' pays you back…for what you've done to me."

When his last nerve snapped, he rounded on her. "You want to get ugly, you got it. Get out or I won't only make you wish you'd never seen me, but that you'd never been born."

His threat had no effect on her; her eyes remained dead.

Then, as if fearing she'd fall apart, she turned and exited the room.

He waited until a muted thud told him she'd left. Then he allowed the pain to overwhelm him.

One

Vincenzo Arsenio D'Agostino stared at his king and reached the only logical conclusion.

The man had lost his mind.

He must have buckled under the pressure of ruling Castaldini while steering his multibillion-dollar business empire. *And* being the most adoring and attentive husband and father who walked the planet. No man could possibly weather all that with his mental faculties intact.

That must be the explanation for what he'd just said.

Ferruccio Selvaggio-D'Agostino—the bastard king, as his opponents called him, relishing it being a literal slur, since Ferruccio *was* an illegitimate D'Agostino—twisted his lips. "Do pick your jaw off the floor, Vincenzo. And no, I'm *not* insane. Get. A. Wife. ASAP."

Dio. He'd said it again.

This time Vincenzo found himself echoing it. "Get a wife."

Ferruccio nodded. *"ASAP."*

"Stop *saying* that."

Mockery gleamed in Ferruccio's steel eyes. "You've got only yourself to blame for the rush. I've needed you on this job for *years,* but every time I bring you up to the council they go apoplectic. Even Leandro and Durante wince when your name is mentioned. That playboy image you've been diligently cultivating is now so notorious, even gossip columns are beginning to play it down. And that image won't cut it in the leagues I need you to play in now."

"That image never hurt *you.* Just look where you are today. The king of one of the most conservative kingdoms in the world, with the purest woman on earth as your queen."

Ferruccio shrugged amusedly at his summation. "I was only known as the 'Savage Ironman' in reference to my name and business reputation, and my reported…hazard to women was beyond wildly exaggerated. I had no time for women as I clawed my way up from the gutter to the top, then I was in love with Clarissa for six years before she became mine. But your notoriety as one of the world's premier womanizers won't do when you're Castaldini's emissary to the United Nations. You've got to clean up your act and spray on some respectability to clear away the stench of the scandals that hang around you."

Vincenzo scowled up at him. "If it's depriving you of sleep, I'll tone things down. But I certainly won't 'get a wife' to appease some political fossils, aka your council. And I won't join your, Leandro's and Durante's trio of henpecked husbands. You're all just jealous you can't have my lifestyle."

Ferruccio gave him that look. The one that made Vincenzo feel hollow inside, made him feel like putting his fist through his king's too-well-arranged face. It was the pitying glance

of a man who knew bone-deep contentment and found nothing more pathetic than Vincenzo's said lifestyle.

"When you're representing Castaldini, Vincenzo, I want
the media only to cover your achievements on behalf of the
kingdom, not your conquests' surgical enhancements or tell-
alls after you exchange them for different models. I don't want
the sensitive diplomatic and economic agendas you'll be negotiating to be overshadowed or even derailed by the media
circus your lifestyle generates. A wife will show the world
that you've changed your ways and will keep the news on the
relevant work you'll be doing."

Vincenzo shook his head in disbelief. "*Dio!* When did you
become such a stick in the mud, Ferruccio?"

"If you mean when did I become an advocate for marriage
and family life, where have you been the last four years? I'm
the living, breathing ad for both. And it's time I did you the
favor of shoving you onto that path."

"What path? The one to happily ever after? Don't you
know that's a mirage most men pursue to no avail? Don't
you realize you've beaten impossible odds in finding Clarissa? That not a man in a million will find a fraction of the
perfection you share with her?"

Ferruccio pursed his lips. "I don't know about those odds,
Vincenzo. Durante found Gabrielle. Leandro found Phoebe."

"Only two more flukes. You all had such terrible things
happen during your childhoods and youths, unbelievably good
stuff has been happening later in life in compensation. Having lived a blessed life early on, I seem to be destined to have
nothing good from now on, to even out the cosmic balance. I
will never find anything like the love you all have."

"You're doing everything in your power *not* to find love,
or to let it find you—"

Vincenzo interrupted him. "I've only accepted my fate.
Love is not in the cards for me."

"And that's *exactly* why I want you to get a wife," Ferruccio interrupted back. "I don't want you to spend your life without the warmth and intimacy, the allegiance and certainty only a good marriage can bring."

"Thanks for the sentiment. But I can't have any of that."

"Because you haven't found love? Love *is* a plus, but not a must. Just look at your parents' example. They started out suitable in theory and turned out right for each other in practice. Pick someone cerebrally and once she's your wife, the qualities that logically appealed to you will weave a bond between you that will strengthen the longer you are together."

"Isn't that an inverted way of doing things? You loved Clarissa first."

"I thought I did, with everything in me. But what I felt for her was a fraction of what I feel for her now. Going by my example, if you start out barely liking your wife, after a year of marriage you'll be ready to die for her."

"Why don't you just acknowledge that you're the luckiest bastard alive, Ferruccio? You may be my king and I may have sworn allegiance to you, but it's not good for your health to keep shoving your happiness in my face when I already told you there's no chance I'll find anything like it."

"I, too, once believed I had no chance at happiness, either, that emotionally, spiritually, I'd remain vacant, with the one woman I wanted forever out of reach while I was incapable of settling for another."

Was Ferruccio just counterarguing with his own example? Or was he putting two and two together and realizing why Vincenzo was so adamant that he'd never find love?

Suddenly, bitterness and dejection ambushed him as if they'd never subsided.

Ferruccio went on, "But you're pushing forty…"

"I'm thirty-eight!"

"...*and* you've been alone since your parents died two *decades* ago..."

"I'm not alone. I have friends."

"*Whom* you don't have time for and who don't have time for you." Ferruccio raised his hand, aborting Vincenzo's interjection. "Make a new family, Vincenzo. It's the best thing you can do for yourself, and incidentally, for the kingdom."

"Next you'll dictate the wife I should 'get.'"

"If you don't decide on one on your own, *ASAP,* I will."

Vincenzo snorted. "Is that crown you've been wearing for the last four years too tight? Or is your head getting bigger? Or is it the mind-scrambling domestic bliss?"

Ferruccio just smiled that inexorable smile of his.

Knowing the kind of laserlike determination Ferruccio had, Vincenzo knew there was no refusing him.

Might as well give in. To an extent he found acceptable. He sighed. "If I take the position..."

"*If* implies this is a negotiation, Vincenzo. It isn't."

"...it will be only for a year..."

"It will be until I say."

"A *year.* This isn't up for negotiation, either. There will be no more 'scandals' in the rags, so this wife thing..."

Ferruccio gave him his signature discussion-ending smile. "Is also nonnegotiable. 'Get a wife' wasn't a suggestion or a request. It's a royal decree."

Ferruccio had eventually buckled. On Vincenzo's one-year proviso. Provided that Vincenzo chose and trained his replacement to *his* satisfaction.

He hadn't budged on the "get a wife" stipulation. He'd even made it official. Vincenzo still couldn't believe what he was looking at. A royal edict ruling that Vincenzo must choose a suitable woman and marry her within two months.

This deserved an official letter from his own corporation telling Ferruccio not to hold his regal breath.

There was no way he'd choose a "suitable woman." Not in two months or two decades. There was no suitable woman for him. Like Ferruccio, he'd been a one-woman man. Unlike him, he'd blown his one shot on an illusion. After six years of being unable to muster the least interest in any other woman he was resigned to his condition.

Though he knew *resigned* wasn't the word for it. Not when every time her memory sank its inky tentacles into his mind, his muscles felt as if they'd snap.

He braced himself until this latest attack passed....

A realization went off in his head like a solar flare.

All these years...he'd been going about it all wrong!

Fighting what he felt with every breath had been the worst thing he could have done. After he'd realized none of it was going away, he should have done the opposite. He should have let it run its course, until it was purged from his system.

But it didn't matter that he hadn't done that before. Now was the perfect time to do it. And to let all those still-seething emotions work to his advantage for once.

A smile tugged at his lips, fueled by what he hadn't felt in six years, what he'd thought he'd never feel again. Excitement. Anticipation. Drive. Challenge.

All he needed now were some updates on Glory to use in this acquisition. He already had enough to make it a hostile takeover, but more leverage wouldn't hurt.

Wouldn't hurt *him*.

Now, *her*—that was a totally different story.

Glory Monaghan stared dazedly at her laptop screen.

She couldn't be seeing this. An email from *him*.

She drew a shaky hand across numb lips, shock reverberating in her every nerve.

Slow down. Think. It must be an old one….

No. This was new. She'd deleted his old emails. Though she had only two months ago. And by accident, too.

Yep, for six years, those emails had migrated from one computer to another with all of her vital data. She hadn't clicked a mouse to scrub her life clean of his degrading echoes. She hadn't gotten rid of one shred of him. Not his scribbled notes, voice messages or anything he'd given her or left at her place.

It *hadn't* been as pathetic as it sounded. It had been therapeutic. Educational. To analyze the mementos and the events associated with each, to familiarize herself further with the workings of the mind of a unique son of a bitch.

The lessons gained from such in-depth scrutiny had been invaluable. No one had ever come close to fooling her again. No one had come close again, period. No one had surprised her, let alone shocked her, since.

Leave it to that royal bastard to be the one to do it.

She resisted the urge to blink in hope that his email would disappear. She did squeeze her eyes, but opened them to find it still staring back at her. His unread message, somehow bolder and blacker than the other unread ones. As if taunting her.

The subject line read An Offer You Can't Refuse.

Incredulity swept inside her like a tornado.

But wait! Why was she thinking it was an actual email from Vincenzo? Some spammer with some lewd scam must have hacked into his account. Yeah. That was it. With a subject line like that, this had to be the only explanation.

Still…it was strange that Vincenzo hadn't deleted her from his list of contacts.

Whatever. This email belonged in the trash.

But before she emptied it, her hand froze on the button, an

internal voice warning, *Do that and go nuts wondering what that email was really all about.*

Okay. She had to concede that point. Knowing herself, she wouldn't be able to function today if she didn't know for sure.

But what if she opened it, only to find some nasty surprise? In the name of her quest for peace of mind, she should delete the damn thing.

God. That bastard was reaching through time and space, tugging at her like a marionette. Just an email with an inflammatory subject line had her spiraling down a vortex of agitation as if she'd never exited it.

Maybe she never had. Maybe she'd only been bottling it up, pretending to be back to normal. Maybe she did need some blow to jolt her out of her simulated animation. Maybe if this *was* an email from him, it would trigger some true resolution so she'd bury his memory once and for all.

She clicked open the email.

Her gaze flew to the bottom. There was a signature. His. This *was* from him.

All the beats her heart had been holding back spilled out in a jumbled outpour. And that was before she read the two sentences that comprised the message.

I can send your family to prison for life, but I'm willing to negotiate. Be at my penthouse at 5:00 p.m., or I'll turn the evidence I have in to the authorities.

At ten to five, Glory was on her way up to Vincenzo's penthouse, déjà vu settling on her like a suffocating cloak.

Her dry-as-sand eyes panned around the elevator she'd once taken almost every day for six months. The memories felt like they belonged to someone else's life.

Which wasn't too far-fetched. She'd been someone else then. After a lifetime of devoting her every waking hour to excelling in her studies, she'd reached the ripe age of twenty-three with zero social skills and the emotional maturity of someone a decade younger. She'd been aware of that, but hadn't had time to work on anything but her intellectual growth. She'd been determined she wouldn't have the life her family had, one of precarious gambles and failed opportunity hunting. She'd wanted a life of stability.

She'd worked to that end since she'd been a teenager, forgoing the time dump others called a social life. And she'd believed she'd been achieving her goal, graduating at the top of her class and obtaining a master's degree with the highest honors. Everyone had projected she'd rise to the top of her field.

But though she'd been confident her outstanding qualifications and recommendations would afford her a high-paying and prestigious job, she'd applied for a position in D'Agostino Developments not really expecting to get it. Not after she'd heard such stories about the man at the helm of the meteorically rising enterprise. In his corporation, Vincenzo D'Agostino had grueling standards. He interviewed and vetted even the mailroom staff. Then he had vetted her.

She still remembered every second of that fateful meeting that had changed her life.

His scrutiny had been denuding, his focus scorching, his questions rapid-fire and deconstructing. His influence had rocked her to her core, making her feel like a swooning moron as she'd sluggishly answered his brusque questions. But after only ten minutes, he'd risen, shaken her hand and given her a much more strategic position than she'd dared hope for, working at the highest level, directly with him.

She'd exited his office reeling at the shock of it all. She hadn't known it was possible for a human being to be so beautiful, so overpowering. She hadn't known a man could have her hot and wet just looking at her across a desk. She hadn't even been interested in a man before, so the intensity of her desire after one meeting had had her in a free fall of confusion.

But while she'd gotten a job she'd thought impossible, she'd thought the real impossibility would be him. Even if he hadn't had an absolute rule against mixing work and pleasure, she couldn't imagine he'd be interested in someone like her. Cerebrally, she knew she was pretty, but a man like him had stunning and sophisticated women swarming all over him, and she'd certainly been neither. Something he'd confirmed when he kicked her out of his life.

She'd been determined to stifle her fantasies so she wouldn't compromise her fantastic position. At least she had until he'd called an hour later, inviting her out to dinner.

Silencing her misgivings about his change of M.O. and its probable negative effects on her career, she stumbled over herself saying yes. She'd thrown discretion to the wind and hurtled full force into his arms, allowing her existence to revolve around him on every level, personal and professional.

Yeah, she'd hurtled all the way off the cliff of his cruelty and exploitation. And she could only blame herself. No law, natural or human-made, protected fools from their folly.

But there'd been one thing she'd learned from that ordeal. Vincenzo didn't joke. Ever. He was as serious as the plague.

In her eyes, it had been the one thing missing from his character back then. Of course, her eyes had been so filled with the plethora of his godlike attributes, she'd given the deficiency nothing but a passing regret. But that fact forced one belief on her. His email had been no prank.

She'd reached that conclusion minutes after she'd read it. After the first shock had passed, she'd gone through the range of extreme reactions until only rage remained.

A ping yanked her out of her murderous musings.

Forcing stiff legs to move, she stepped out into the hall leading to that royal slimeball's floor-spanning penthouse.

Nothing had changed. Which was weird. She'd thought he would have remodeled the whole building to suit the changing trends and his inflating status and wealth.

He'd once told her this opulent edifice in the heart of New York was nothing compared to his family home in Castaldini. He'd pretended he couldn't wait to take her there. His desire to take her there, and the prospect of visiting his home, had kept her in a state of constant anticipation and excitement.

But she hadn't been able to imagine anything more lavish than this place. His whole world had made her feel what Alice must have felt when she'd fallen into Wonderland. It *had* alerted her to how radically different they were, how it made no sense that they'd come together. But she'd ignored reason.

Until he'd thrown her out of his life like so much garbage.

Another wave of fury crashed over her as she stopped at his door.

He must be watching her through the security camera. He always had, barely letting her enter before sweeping her away on the rapids of his eagerness. Or so she'd thought.

She glared up at where the camera was hidden. She still had the key. Another memento she hadn't thrown away. He probably hadn't changed the lock. Why should he have? With enough guards to stop an army, she wouldn't have gotten here without his permission.

He probably expected her to ring the bell. Yeah, right. He might have dragged her here, but she was damned if he'd leave her waiting until he deigned to open the door.

She stabbed the key in, imagining the lock was his eye.

Her breath still hitched as the door clicked open, then again as she stepped inside.

He stood facing her at the end of the expansive sitting area, in front of the screen where he'd once displayed their video-taped sessions of sexual delirium as he'd drowned her in more.

Her heart clamored out of control as his steel-hued eyes struck her with a million volts of sexiness and charisma across the distance.

He'd once been the epitome of male beauty. Now he'd become impossibly more, his influence enhanced, his assets augmented.

Dressed in all black, he seemed taller than his six foot five, his shoulders even wider, his waist and hips sparser in comparison to a torso and thighs that had bulked up with muscle. His face was hewn to sharper planes and angles, his skin a darker, silkier copper, intensifying the luminescence of his eyes. The discreet silver brushing his luxurious raven hair at the temples added the last touch of allure.

But she wasn't only checking off his upgrades against what she'd known…too intimately. She was reacting to him in the same way, with the same intensity she had when she'd been younger, inexperienced and oblivious of his reality.

Weird, this disconnect between mental aversion and physical affinity.

She could barely breathe, and that was before he spoke, his voice deeper, strumming hidden places inside her with each inflection, with that trace accent, those rolling *r*'s…

"Before you say anything, yes, I do have evidence that would send your father and brother to prison from fifteen to life. But you must already be certain of that. That's why you're here."

Her momentary incapacitation cracked.

She moved steadily toward him, roiling rage fueling each step. "I know you're capable of anything. *That's* why I'm here."

His eyes smoldered as they documented her state. "I'll

dispense with the preliminaries then and get to the point of my summons."

She stopped feet away, scoffing, "Summons? Wow. Your 'princehood' has gone to your head, hasn't it? But then, you must have always been this pompous and loathsome, and I was the one who was too blind to notice."

Those sculpted lips that had once driven her to insanity twisted. "I don't have time now for your scorned-woman barbs, Glory. But once my objective is fulfilled, I might accommodate your need to vent. It will be…amusing."

Bringing herself under control, she matched his coolness. "I'm sure it will be. Sharks do relish blood. And that, along with anything I say to you or about you, isn't a barb. Just a fact. So let's stop wasting calories and get to the point of your 'summons.' What will it take so you won't destroy my family? If you want me to steal some top secret info from your rivals, I no longer work in your field, as I'm sure you know."

An imperious eyebrow rose. "Would you have, if you were?"

Her answer was unhesitating. "No."

Something streaked in his eyes, something that looked like…pain? What made it even more confusing was that it was tinged with…humor? Humor? Vincenzo? And now of all times?

"Not even to save your beloved family?"

She wanted to growl that they were no such thing.

Oh, sure, she loved them. But they drove her up the wall being so irresponsible. They were why she was now at this royal scumbag's mercy. He must have acquired some debts of theirs. And if he could send them to prison using those, they must be *huge*.

"No," she said, more forcefully this time. "I was just analyzing the only thing you might think I have to offer in return for your generous amnesty."

"That's not the only thing you have to offer."

For heart-scrambled moments it felt as if he meant…

No. No way. He'd told her in mutilating detail what an exchangeable "lay" she'd been. He'd discarded her and moved on to a thousand others. And he was known to never return to an already pollinated flower. He wouldn't go to these lengths, or any, to have her in his bed again.

Her glare grew harder. "I *can* offer you a much deserved skull fracture. Apart from that, I can't think of a thing."

This time, the humor filling his eyes and lips was unmistakable, shaking her more than anything else had.

"I'll pass on the kind cranial-reconstruction offer. But there is another alteration you can offer me that I vitally need." His lips quirked as if at a private joke. "ASAP."

"Will you stop wasting my time and just spit it out? What the hell do you 'need'?"

Unfazed by her fury, he calmly said, "A wife."

Two

"A wife?"

Glory heard herself echoing what Vincenzo had said.

But he couldn't have said *that*.

He only nodded, confirming that she'd parroted him correctly.

Dazed, she shook her head. "How can I offer you a wife?" A suspicion hit her between the eyes. "You're interested in someone I know?"

That lazy humor heated his eyes again. "Yes. Someone you know very well."

Nausea twisted her stomach as every woman she knew flashed through her mind. Many were beautiful and sophisticated enough to qualify for Vincenzo's demanding standards. Amelia, her best friend, in particular. But she was newly engaged. Was that why Vincenzo had her here, because he wanted her help to break up her friend's relationship so he'd…?

He interrupted the apoplectic fit in progress. "According to my king, I need an emergency reputation upgrade that only a wife can provide."

Her mind burned rubber calibrating the new info. "Your sexual exploits are giving Castaldini a bad name? That must be why King Ferruccio had to intervene. Did he issue you a royal decree to cease and desist?"

He gave a tranquil nod of that leonine head of his. "What amounted to that, *si*. That's why I'm 'getting a wife.'"

"Who knew? Even the untouchable Vincenzo D'Agostino has someone he bows down to. It must have stung bad, standing before another man, even if he is your lord and liege, being chastised like a kid and told what to do, huh? How does it feel to be forced to end your stellar career as a womanizer?"

One of those formidable shoulders jerked nonchalantly. "I'm ending nothing. I'm only getting a wife temporarily."

So he wasn't even pretending he'd change his ways. At least no one could accuse him of hiding what he was. No one but her. He'd hidden his nature and intentions ingeniously for the duration of their…liaison—what he'd made her believe had been a love affair to rival those of literature and legend.

She exhaled her rising frustration. "Of course she'd have to be temporary. All the power and money in the world, which you do have, wouldn't get you a woman permanently."

His uncharacteristic amusement singed her again. "You're saying women wouldn't fall over themselves to marry me?"

"Oh, I bet there'd be queues across the globe panting at the prospect. What I'm saying is any woman would end up paying whatever price to get rid of you once she got to know the real you. There's no way a woman would want you for life."

"Isn't it lucky then that I don't want one for anywhere near that long? I just need a woman who'll follow every rule of my temporary arrangement to the letter. But my problem isn't in finding the woman who'll accept my terms. It would be difficult to find one who won't."

"You're that conceited, you think all women would be so desperate for you, they'd accept you on any terms, no matter how short-lived and degrading?"

"That's not conceit. That's a fact. You being a case in point. You accepted me on no terms whatsoever. *And* clung so hard, I ended up needing to pull your tentacles out of my flesh with more harshness than I've ever had to employ before or since."

She stared at him, shriveling with remembered shame and again wondered…why all this malice? This fluency of abuse? When all she'd ever done was lose her mind over him.…

He went on, his eyes cold. "But any woman, once she's carrying my name, might use my need to keep up appearances, the reason that drove me to marriage in the first place, to milk the situation for more. I need someone who can't even think it."

"Just hire a…mercenary then," she hissed. "One practiced enough to pretend to stand you, for a fixed time and price."

"A…mercenary is exactly what I'm after. But one who's not overtly…experienced. I need someone who's maintained an outwardly pristine reputation. I am trying to polish mine, after all, and it wouldn't do to put a chipped jewel in my already tarnished crown."

"Even an actual immaculate gem would fail to improve your gaudiness. But you should have called ahead. I certainly don't know anyone, well or not, who fits the category of… mercenary, let alone one so…experienced she simulates a spotless past. I don't even know someone reckless or desperate enough to accept you on any terms, for any length of time."

"You do know someone who fits all those criteria. You."

Vincenzo watched Glory as his last word drained every bit of blood and expression from her face. The face that had haunted him for six years. It was still the same, yet so different.

The last plumpness had vanished, exposing a bone structure that was a masterpiece of exquisiteness. It brought her every feature into stark focus, in a display of harmony and gorgeousness. Her complexion, due to her new outdoorsy lifestyle, was tanned a perfect honey, only shades lighter than her magnificent waterfall of tawny hair. Her skin gleamed with health, stretching taut over those elegant bones. Her eyebrows were denser, their arch defined and decisive, her nose more refined, more authoritative and her jaw cleaner, stronger.

But it was still those summer skies she had for eyes that struck him to his core. And those flushed lips. They looked fuller, as if they'd absorbed what had been chiseled off her cheeks. They were more sensuous even in their current severity. Just looking at them made every part of him they'd once worshipped and owned tense, tingle, clamor for their touch. Everything about her had him fighting to ease an arousal that had hardened to steel. And that was before his appraisal traveled down to her body.

That body that had held the code to his libido.

It was painfully clear it still did, now more than ever. But while her face had been chiseled, her body had filled out, the enhanced curves making her the epitome of toned femininity, a woman just hitting the stride of her allure and vigor. Her newly physical lifestyle really agreed with her.

Her navy pantsuit was designed to obscure her assets, but he had X-ray vision where she was concerned. And he couldn't wait until he confirmed his estimates with an unhindered visual and hands-on examination.

For now, he just wondered how those eyes of hers didn't display any tinge of the cunning the woman who'd once set him up should have. They only transmitted the indomitable edge of a warrior used to fighting adversaries who surpassed her in power a hundredfold. As she knew he did.

Or, at least they had until he'd said "You."

Her eyes now displayed nothing but absolute shock. If he didn't know better, he'd think she hadn't even considered that he'd been talking about her.

But of course she had. She was just in a class of her own when it came to spontaneous acting.

She blinked, as if coming out of a trance, shock giving way to fury so icy it burned him. "I don't care how big a debt my father and brother have. I'll pay it off."

He didn't see *that* coming. "You think what I have on them is a debt? You really think I'd have leverage so lame it could be nullified with money?"

"Quit posturing, you loathsome jerk. What *do* you have on them?"

He paused, testing, even tasting, his reaction to her insult. It felt like exhilaration, tasted tart and zesty. He immediately wanted more.

Dio. If he was hankering for more of her slurs, he must be queasier than he thought with all the deference he got in his official and professional roles. Not that he could imagine himself reveling in anybody else's verbal abuse.

His lips tugged as he contemplated his newfound desire to be bashed by her, knowing it would inflame her more. Which was just what he was after. "Oh, just a few crimes."

Her jaw dropped. "You'd go as far as framing them to get me to do your bidding?"

"I'm just exposing them. And only a fraction of their crimes at that. To save posturing on *your* end, read this." He bent, swiped a dossier off the coffee table between them and held it out to her. "Verify my evidence any way you like. I have more if you want. But that would be overkill. This is quite enough to see both in prison for embezzlement and fraud for maybe the rest of your father's life, and most of what's left of your brother's."

Her hand rose as if without volition, receiving the dossier. With one more dazed look, she relinquished his gaze, turned unsteadily and sank down onto the couch where he'd once taken her. He'd made love to her in every corner of this place. At least, *he'd* been making love. Love, or anything genuine, hadn't been involved on her end.

He watched her as she leafed through the pages with unsteady hands, that amazing speed-reading ability engaged, letting memories sweep through him at last.

How he'd loved her. Now he needed to exorcise her.

It felt as if hours had passed before she raised her gaze back to his, her eyes reddened, her lips trembling. What an incredible simulation of disbelief and devastation.

When she talked, her voice was thick and hoarse, as if she were barely holding back tears. "How long have you had… that?"

"That particular accumulation of damning evidence? Over a year. I have much older files retracing the rest of their crimes, in case you're interested."

"There was more?"

Anyone looking at her would swear this was the shock of her life, that she'd never suspected the men in her family could possibly be involved in criminal activities.

He huffed his disgust at the whole situation, and everyone involved in it. "They're both extremely good, I'll give them that. That's why no one else has caught them at it yet."

"Why have you?"

She was asking all the right questions. If he answered them all truthfully, they'd paint her the real picture of what had happened in the past. Which wouldn't be a bad idea. He was sick and tired of the pretense.

So he told her. "I've been keeping them under close scrutiny since the attempts to steal my research."

Her eyes rounded in renewed shock. "You suspected them?"

"I suspected everyone with access to me, direct or indirect."

A stricken look entered her eyes, as if she was just now realizing he must have suspected her, too. Of course, she was still under the impression that nothing of value had been stolen. When everything had been.

It had been so sensitive, even with all his security, he'd documented his results in bits and pieces that only he could put together. But they'd still been accessed and reconstructed and appeared in the hands of his rivals. Then he'd been given proof that the breach had originated from Glory.

But he'd insisted it must have been someone who had total access to Glory. Only her family had that. Needing to settle this without her knowledge, only thinking of her heartache if she found out, he'd confronted them. They'd broken under his threats, begged his leniency. He'd already decided to show them that, for Glory, but he'd said he'd only consider it if they gave him the details of their plan, their recruiters and any accomplices. If they didn't, he'd show no mercy. And they'd given him proof that it had been Glory. She'd been their only hope of getting to him.

And how she'd gotten to him.

She'd played him like a virtuoso. It hadn't even occurred to him to guard himself against her like he did with everyone else.

But a lengthy, highly publicized court case would have harmed more than helped him. Worse, it would have kept her in his life. So he'd groped for the lesser mutilation of cutting her off from his life abruptly, so the sordid mess wouldn't get any bigger.

Then something totally unexpected had happened. Also because of her.

As he'd struggled to put her out of his mind, he'd restarted his work from scratch, soon becoming thankful he had. What he'd thought was a breakthrough had actually been fundamentally flawed. If he hadn't lost the whole thing, he would have cost his sponsors untold billions of wasted development financing. But the real catastrophe would have been if the magnitude of confidence in his research had minimized testing before its applications hit the market. Lives could have been lost.

So her betrayal had been a blessing in disguise, forcing him to correct his mistakes and devise a safe, more cost-effective and streamlined method. After that, he'd been catapulted to the top of his field. Not that he was about to thank Glory for the betrayal that had led to all that.

Glory's choking words brought him out of the darkness of the past. "But they had nothing to do with your leaked research. And according to you, there *was* no leaked research."

"Not for lack of trying on the culprits' part. That I placed false results for them to steal doesn't exonerate them from the crime of industrial espionage and patent theft."

Her sluggish nod conceded that point. "But if you didn't pursue them then, they must have checked out. So why did you keep them under a microscope all this time?"

So she was still playing the innocence card. Fine. He'd play it her way. He had a more important goal now than exhuming past corpses. He'd get closure in a different way, which wouldn't involve exposing the truth. If she still believed she'd failed in her mission, he'd let her keep thinking that.

His lips twisted on ever-present bitterness. "What can I say? I follow my gut. And it told me they were shifty, and to keep an eye on them. Since I could easily afford to, I did. And because I was already following their every move, I found out each instance when they stepped out of line, even when others couldn't. I also learned their methods, so I could anticipate them. They didn't stand a chance."

A long moment of silence passed, filled with the world of hurt and disillusion roiling in her eyes.

Then she rasped, "Why haven't you reported them?"

Because they're your family.

There. He'd finally admitted it to himself.

Something that felt like a boulder sitting on his chest suddenly lifted. He felt as if he could breathe fully again, after years of only snatching in enough air to survive.

So this was how it felt to be free of self-deceptions.

It *had* sat heavily on his conscience, that he'd known of her family's habitual crimes and not done anything about it. He'd tried to rationalize why he hadn't, but it had boiled down to this: after all she'd done to him, he still hadn't been able to bring himself to damage her to that extent. He had been unable to cause her the loss of her family, as shoddy as they were. But even more, he couldn't have risked that they might have implicated her.

In spite of everything, he hadn't been able to contemplate sending her to prison.

Not that he was about to let her realize that she'd always had control over every irrational cell in his body.

He gave her one of the explanations he'd placated himself with. "I didn't see any benefit to myself or to my business in doing so." At her widening stare, he huffed. "I'm not just a mad scientist, not anymore. And then, scientists are among the most ruthless pragmatists around. Since the incidents six years ago, I've learned it always pays to have some dirt on everyone, to use when needed. Now the time has come for that nugget to deliver its full potential."

"And you think you can coerce me into marrying you, even temporarily, using their crimes?"

"Yes. It would make you the perfect temporary wife. You're the only woman who wouldn't be tempted to ask for more at the end of the contract's terms, or risk any kind of scandal."

Another silence detonated in the wake of his final taunt.

With eyes brimming, she sat up and tossed her head, making her shimmering hair shift to one side with an audible hiss.

He struggled not to swoop down on her, harness her by those luxurious tresses, ravage those lush lips, crush that voluptuousness under his weight and take her, make her writhe her pleasure beneath him, pour all of his inside her.

She exacerbated his condition with the lash of her challenge. "What if I told you I don't care what you do with said 'nugget'? If they did the things this file says they did, then they deserve to be locked up to pay for their crimes, and learn a lesson nothing else could teach them."

Elation at her defiance and disgust at the whole situation mingled in an explosive mix, almost making him lightheaded. "They may deserve it, but you still won't let them get locked up for a day, let alone years, if you can at all help it."

All anger and rebellion went out of her, dejection crashing in its place. Her shoulders slumped and her eyes dimmed.

He attempted to look unaffected by her apparent upheaval and defeat. *Apparent* being the operative word. In reality she must be rubbing her hands at the unexpected windfall and what she could negotiate out of it.

He exhaled. "It's a beneficial arrangement all around. Though your father and brother deserve to be punished, their punishment wouldn't serve any purpose. I…will compensate those they've embezzled from and defrauded." He'd nearly slipped and told her that he'd *already* compensated their victims, each in a way that made up for their losses, without connecting his actions to those, or to her family. "You will be spared the disgrace and heartache of having them imprisoned. My king and Castaldini will have me where they need me. And I will have the temporary image cleansing necessary for the job."

Her gaze froze on his face for a fraught moment until his heart started to thunder in his chest. And that was before a couple of tears arrowed down her flushed, trembling cheeks.

She wiped them away, as if pissed off with herself for letting him witness her weakness. Her turmoil seemed so real he felt it reverberating in his bones. But it couldn't be real. It had to be another act. But how could it be so convincing?

He should stop wondering. As far as his senses were concerned, her every breath and word and look were genuine. So he'd better stop pitting their verdict against that of his mind before they tore him down the middle in their tug-of-war.

She finally whispered, "How temporary is temporary?"

He exhaled heavily. "A year."

Her face convulsed as if at a stab of pain.

After swallowing with evident difficulty, she asked, "What would be the…job description?"

So she'd moved from rejection to defiance to setting terms. And somehow, though he was holding all the cards, it felt like she was the one setting the pace of this confrontation, steering its direction. No wonder. She'd been the best negotiator he'd ever had on his team, the most ordered, effective executive. He *had* loved her for her mind and abilities as much as everything else. He'd respected them, believed in them. Relied on them. Her loss had damaged every pillar in his world.

Pushing aside the bitterness that kept derailing him, he said, "I will be Castaldini's representative to the United Nations. It's one of the most exalted positions in the kingdom, and it is closely monitored and rated by Castaldinians before the rest of the world. My wife will need to share all of my public appearances, act as the proper consort in all the functions I attend, the gracious hostess in the ones I give, and the adoring bride in everything else."

Her incredulity rose with his every word. "And you think I am qualified for those roles? Why don't you just get someone from Castaldini, a minor princess or something, who'd jump at the chance for a temporary place in the spotlight, and who's been trained from birth in royal and diplomatic pretense? I'm sure no woman will cling or cause scandals when you want to cast her aside. You cast me aside without as much as a wrinkle in your suit."

No. Just a chasm in my heart. "I want no one else. And yes, you are qualified and then some. You're an unequaled expert in all aspects of the executive life with its due process and formalities. You're also quite the chameleon, and you blend perfectly in any situation or setting." Her eyes widened at that, as if she'd never heard anything more ridiculous in her life. Before she could voice her derision, he went on. "The jump to court and diplomatic etiquette and 'pretense' should be a breeze. I will tutor you in what you'll say and how you'll behave with dignitaries and the press. I'll leave the other areas of your education to Alonzo, my valet. And with your unusual beauty, and your…assets—" his gaze made an explicit sweep of said assets before returning to her once again chagrined eyes "—once Alonzo gets his hands on you, the tabloids will have nothing to talk about but your style and latest outfits. Your current occupation as a humanitarian crusader will also capture the imagination of the world, and add to my image as a clean-energy pioneer. We'll be the perfect fairy-tale couple."

What he'd once thought they could be for real.

His summation seemed to have as brutal an effect on her as it had on him. She looked as if regret that this could never be real crushed her, too.

Suppressing the urge to put his fist through the nearest wall, he gritted out, "I am also offering a substantial financial incentive to sweeten the deal. That's part of the offer I've already said you can't refuse."

She kept staring at him with what looked like disappointment pulsing in the depths of her eyes. She didn't ask how much. Still acting as if money meant nothing to her.

"Ten million dollars," he said, suppressing a sneer of disillusion. "Net of deductions or taxes. Two up front, the rest on completion of the contract term."

He bent, picked up the other dossier on the coffee table and came to stand over her where she sat limply on the couch. "That's the prenuptial agreement you'll sign."

When she didn't take the volume, he placed it on her lap.

"I'm giving you today to read through this. You're free to seek legal counsel, of course, but there's nothing in it to impact you whatsoever, if you abide by the letter of the terms. I will expect your acceptance tomorrow."

Without looking up from the dossier in her lap, she said, "Take it or take it, huh?"

"That about sums it up."

The gaze fixed on his filled with fury, frustration and... vulnerability.

Dio. Just a look from her and his whole being surged with need. To devour her, to possess her. To protect her.

Seemed his weakness where she was concerned was incurable.

And to think he'd hoped he'd realize that everything he'd felt for her was an exaggeration, that seeing her again would only make him wonder at how he'd once thought himself attracted to her. He'd hoped it would purge the memories that circulated in his system like a nondegradable mind-altering drug.

Instead, he'd found that what he remembered of her effect on him had been diluted by time. Either that or her effect had multiplied tenfold. He'd been aroused since he'd laid eyes on her again, was now in agony.

His only consolation was that she wanted him, too.

Si, of this he had no doubt. Not even she could have faked her body's responses. Their memory had controlled his fantasies all these years. Every manifestation of her desire, the scent of it, the taste of its honey on his tongue, the feel of its liquid silk on his fingers and manhood, the rush of her pleasure at the peaks that had rocked her beneath him, squeezed her around him and wrung him of explosive releases.

What would it feel like having her again with all their baggage, maturity and changes?

No need to wonder. For he'd made up his mind.

He *would* have her again.

Might as well make his intentions clear up front.

He caught her arm as she heaved up. Jolts arced from every fingertip pressing into firm flesh.

At her indignant glare, he bent and whispered in her ear, "When I take you to my bed this time, it will be far better than ever before."

Her flesh buzzed in his hand, her breath becoming choppy, her pupils dilating. Her scent rose to perfume the air, to fill his lungs with the evidence of her arousal.

Still, she said, "I will never sign to that."

"And I'd never ask you to. This has nothing to do with the deal. You have full freedom on this front. I'm only letting you know I want you in my bed. And you will come. Because you want to. Because you want me."

Her pupils fluctuated, her cheeks flushed. Proof positive of his claims.

She still scoffed, even if in a voice that had deepened to the timbre that used to arouse him out of his mind, as it did now. "You really have to see someone for that head of yours, before it snaps off your neck under its own weight."

He tugged on her arm, brought her slamming against him. A groan escaped him at the glorious feel of her against him from breast to knee. A moan of stimulation issued from her before she could stifle it.

The bouquet that had been tantalizing him since she'd walked in—her unique brand of femininity, that of sunshine-soaked days and pleasure-drenched nights—deluged his lungs. He had to get more, leave no breath unmingled with it.

He buried his face in her neck, inhaled her, absorbing her shudder into his. "I don't want you in my bed. I *need* you there. I've craved you there for six long years."

The body that had gone limp at contact with his stiffened, pushing away only enough to look confusedly up at him.

Feeling he'd said too much, he let her go before he swept her up and carried her to bed here and now.

Her face was a canvas of every turbulent emotion there was, so intense he felt almost dizzy at their onslaught.

And he found himself adding, "Passion was the one real thing we shared. You were the best I've ever had. I only ended it with you because you—" he barely caught back an accusation "—seemed to expect more than was on offer." He injected his voice with nonchalance. "But now you know what is on offer. You have every choice in becoming my lover, but none in being my princess."

Her gaze dropped to the dossier in her hand, which regulated their temporary relationship's boundaries and how it would end with a cold precision he was already starting to question.

Then she raised her eyes, the azure now dull and distant. "Only for a year."

Or longer. As long as we both want, he almost blurted out.

Catching back the impetuousness with all he had, he nodded. "Only for a year."

Three

"How long?"

Glory winced at her best friend's shrill stupefaction.

She was already regretting telling Amelia anything. But Glory had felt her head and heart might explode if she didn't tell someone. And it couldn't have been her mother. Glenda Monaghan would have a breakdown if she knew what her husband and son had been up to. Or what they were in danger of if Glory didn't go through with Vincenzo's "deal." The "take it or I send your family up the river for life" deal.

Glory smirked at her best friend's flabbergasted expression. "Don't you think you're going about this in reverse? You keep asking me a question right after I answer it."

Amelia rolled her long-lashed golden eyes. "Ex*cuse* me, Ms. Monaghan. We'll see how you'll fare when I come to you saying *I* was once on mouth-to-mouth-and-way-more terms with a prince of freaking Castaldini, who happens to be the foremost scientist and businessman in the clean-energy field, and that he now wants to marry me."

"Only for a year," Glory added, her heart twisting again.

Amelia threw her hands, palms up, at her. "There. You've said it again. So don't get prissy with me while I'm in shock. I mean…Vincenzo D'Agostino? Whoa!"

Glory emptied her lungs on a dejected sigh. "Yeah."

Amelia sagged down on the couch beside her. "Man. I'm trying to compose this picture of you with Prince Vastly Devastating himself, and I'm failing miserably."

Glory's exhalation was laced with mockery this time. "Thanks, Amie, so kind of you."

"It's not that I don't think you're on his level!" Amelia exclaimed. "Any man on any level would be lucky to have you look his way. But you haven't been making any XY chromosome carriers lucky since the Ice Age. You've been such a cold fish…." She winced then smiled sheepishly. "You *know* how you are with men. You radiate this 'do not approach or else' vibe. It's impossible to imagine you in the throes of passion with any man. But now I'm realizing your standards are just much higher than us mere mortal women. It's either someone of Vincenzo's caliber or nothing. Or—" realization seemed to hit Amelia, making her eyes drain of lightheartedness, then fill with wariness "—is it because it's Vincenzo or nothing? Is he the one who spoiled you for other men?"

Glory stared at her. She'd never thought of it this way.

After the brutal way Vincenzo had ended their affair, she'd been devastated, emotionally and psychologically. For the next year, she hadn't thought beyond stopping being miserable. After that, she'd poured all of her time and energy into changing her direction in life.

It had taken Vincenzo's kicking her out of his life, and out of her job, to make her realize the fatal flaw in her unwavering quest for security and stability. She'd known then that there could be neither, emotional or financial. If the man she'd thought to be her soul mate could destroy both with a few words, she wouldn't count on anything again. She'd decided to give her heart and skills to the world and hope they'd do it more good than they'd done her.

The more she'd achieved, the more in demand she'd been. For the past five years, she'd been constantly on the go, living out of a suitcase, setting up and streamlining multiple humanitarian operations across the globe. If she'd wanted intimacies, they would have had to be passing encounters. And those just weren't for her.

But now, after Amelia's questions, she had to pause and wonder. Had one of the major attractions of that whole lifestyle been the legitimate and continuous way of escaping intimacies?

Glory loved her job, couldn't ask for anything more fulfilling on a personal or professional level. But it *had* given her no respite, no time or energy for self-reflection or reassessment. Had she unconsciously sought that flat-out pace to make herself too unavailable? Too consumed to even sense anything missing? So she didn't have to face that she'd always be a one-man woman? That for her, it *was* Vincenzo or nothing?

Amelia must have read the answer in Glory's silent stare, for she, too, exhaled. "Did he break your heart?"

"No. He...smashed it."

Amelia frowned, expression darkening. "Okay, now I hate the guy. I saw him a few times on TV, and I don't know how I didn't peg him for a slimeball! I thought he sounded like a pretty decent guy, no airs, and even with his reputation, I remember wondering how he demolished the stereotype of the royal playboy. I thought being a scientist saved him from being a narcissistic monster. But I stand corrected."

The ridiculous urge to defend him overpowered Glory. "He isn't...wasn't like that. He's—he's just... I don't know." She shook her head in confusion. "It's like he's two—no, three people. The man I fell in love with was like you describe him—honorable, sincere and grounded in his public life, focused, driven and brilliant in his working one, and sensitive, caring and passionate in person. Then there was the man who ended things with me, cold and callous, even vicious. And finally there's the man I met today. Relentless and dominating, yet nothing like the man who took everything seriously, or the man who relished humiliating me."

"Humiliating you?" The edge to Amelia's rising fury was a blade against Glory's inflamed nerves. "And now he's asking you to marry him to fix his reputation? And don't say 'only for a year' again or I may have to break something. I can't believe I was excited at first! Tell him to take his short-term-lease-marriage offer and go to hell."

Glory had always thought Amelia as magnificent as a golden lioness. She now looked like one defending her cub. Her reaction warmed Glory even through the ice of her despondency. "You mean you wouldn't have told me to tell him that anyway?"

"No, I wouldn't have. I mean, you're not in the market for a regular marriage anyway, then comes Prince Very Delicious offering you a year in a fairy tale with a ten million dollar cash bonus. If he wasn't a scumbag who seems to have crippled you emotionally for life, I would have thought it a super deal for you. Now what I want to know is how *dare* he approach you of all people with his offer?"

Glory hadn't shared Vincenzo's reason for picking her. As the one "convenient"—not to mention compromised—enough for his needs. Again. She exhaled and escaped answering.

Amelia harrumphed. "But it doesn't matter what he's thinking. If he bothers you after you say no, I'll have my Jack have a word with his teeth."

Imagining Jack, a bear of a man and a bruiser, pitted against the equally powerful but refined great feline Vincenzo suddenly brought a giggle bursting out of her.

Pulling back from the edge of hysteria, Glory's laughter died on a heavy sigh. "I'm not looking for an intervention here, Amie. I only wanted to…share. I—" she barely swallowed back *have to* "—already decided to say yes."

Amelia gaped at her. Glory hadn't told her of Vincenzo's ultimatum, either. If she did, Jack and his whole rugby team would be after Vincenzo. Then Vincenzo would gather all those hulking wonders he had for cousins and it would probably lead to a war between the U.S. and Castaldini.…

She suppressed the mania bubbling inside her, and focused on overriding Amelia's vehement objections. "It'll only be for a year, Amie. And just think what I can do for all the causes I'm involved in with ten million dollars."

Amelia snorted. "Not much. That would barely supply a few clean-water stations. If you're foolish enough to put yourself within range of the man who hurt and humiliated you, I'd ask for a *hundred* million. He can afford it, and he's the one who needs to scrape a mile-deep of dirt from his image with your shining one. At least you'd be risking annihilation for a good enough cause."

Glory smiled weakly at the firebrand she had for a best friend. She'd met Amelia five years ago while working with Doctors Without Borders. They'd hit it off immediately—two women who'd worked all their lives to become professionals, then discovered, each through her own ordeal, that they needed a cause, not a career. As a corporate and international law expert, Amelia had made it possible for Glory to accomplish things she'd thought impossible. Amelia always insisted Glory's business and economic know-how were more valuable than law—in a world where money was a constant when everything else was mercurial.

"I wanted you to take a look at this.…" She reached for the hardcover prenuptial agreement as if reaching for a bomb. She dropped it in Amelia's lap as if it scalded her and attempted a wink. "That's mainly why I told you. To get your legal opinion on this little gem."

Amelia stared at the heavy volume in her lap with the gilded inscription proclaiming its nature. "I'd say this is a huge one. And from the looks and weight of it, I'm not sure *gem* is the right word for it, either. Okay, let's see what Prince Very Disturbing has to offer."

Unable to sit beside her as she read Vincenzo's terms, Glory got up and went to the kitchen.

While she searched for something to do, she tried telling herself that, considering the situation, the prenuptial shouldn't disturb her. She'd never seen one, and she had no knowledge of marriage laws. Maybe this language was standard within every marriage where one party outranks the other in position and wealth a thousandfold.

She wasn't poor, but financial ease had ceased to be a goal to her. She'd settled for having no debts, and a few inexpensive needs. But in comparison to Vincenzo with his Midas touch, she guessed she would rank as destitute. Maybe he had to consider his investors when he dealt with anything that could affect him financially. Maybe even his board of directors had a say in his financial decisions, and in today's world, marriage was one.

But did he have to go that far with the prenup, as if he was safeguarding himself from a hardened criminal? Or was it she who didn't know what was too far?

She'd made apple pie from scratch and baked it by the time Amelia entered the kitchen with the volume tucked beneath her arm, and a thundercloud hanging over her head.

Amelia slammed the prenup on the island with a huff of disgust. "The only thing he left out was the number of cutlery pieces that have to be accounted for before he gives you the 'latter portion of the monetary settlement at termination of contract term'!"

Glory's heart kicked her ribs. "It's that bad, huh?"

"Worse. This guy is making provisions for provisions, as if he's dealing with a repeat offender known for 'stealing kohl from the eye,' like I heard they say in Castaldini."

Just what Glory had been thinking.

Now that Amelia had confirmed her suspicion, her confusion deepened. Why all this? So a man in his position had much to lose, but *he* was forcing her to serve a sentence in lieu of her family. Could he really think she'd want to prolong it, or try to bribe him or cause any trouble at its end?

But those extensive precautions said that he did. Why? Because of her family's history? Didn't he already know she had nothing to do with her father's and brother's actions and choices? With his surveillance and investigations, he must know she'd had very little to do with them in the past years. She maintained close relations with her mother, who had nothing to do with her husband's and son's transgressions and stupidities. Or was Vincenzo just this paranoid with everyone?

He had been very cautious with people in general. She'd thought she'd been the exception, that he'd been totally open and trusting with her. Yeah, sure. Just like she'd thought he'd felt anything for her.

It had all been a lie. A mirage. This was the reality. That he'd never bothered to know anything about her. No, worse, that he thought the worst of her.

Amelia's harrumph brought Glory out of her musings. "You wanted my opinion? Based on a prenup like that, and the rest of this man's pattern of behavior? Go for a *billion* dollars, Glory. Up front. And right after the wedding, go for his balls."

After Amelia had given her verdict on Vincenzo's offer and Vincenzo himself, she'd insisted on going over the "submission contract." She'd spent the rest of the night dissecting it, and writing down in lawyer-speak what Glory would ask for instead. It was past two in the morning by the time Amelia left, and not of her own accord. Glory had to pretend to fall asleep on the couch to convince her she couldn't take anymore.

Not that she'd wanted to sleep. In fact, she'd known sleep would be an impossibility tonight. Maybe every night from now on. As long as Vincenzo was back in her life.

Her sleeping patterns had already been irrevocably changed since she'd first met him. First, with nights of longing, then ones interspersed with repeated lovemaking, then memories and miseries. She'd only had a measure of her old sleeping soundness restored when she'd maintained a schedule that knocked her out for the five or six hours she allotted for rest.

Right now she felt she was back in the bed of thorns of post-Vincenzo devastation. Even worse. Now she was caught in his maelstrom again, in a far more ambiguous relationship than ever before; she felt she was lying on burning coals.

But apart from the shock of her family's crimes and Vincenzo's outrageous "offer," what really shook her were those last minutes at his penthouse.

Everything inside her had surged so fiercely in response, it had incapacitated her. Outraged her. That after all the heartache and humiliation, he only had to touch her, to tell her he wanted her, that she'd been the best he'd ever had, to have her body come to life, proclaiming him its master…

A classic ringtone sundered the stillness of the night.

Jerking up in bed, her heart thundered, unformed dreads deluging her. Her mother. She'd been fragile since her last round of cancer treatments months ago. Something had happened….

She fumbled for the phone, almost dropping it when she

hit the button to answer. A deep-as-night voice poured into her brain.

"Are you awake?"

Gulping down aborted fright, anger flooded in to replace it, dripping into her voice. "It figures. You had to be one of those unfeeling, self-absorbed people who wake up others to ask if they're awake."

Dark amusement tinged his fathomless voice, making her almost see, taste, the smile that tugged at his lips. "You sound awake."

"I am now, thanks to a royal pain."

A bone-liquefying reverberation poured right into her brain, yanking at her responses. "So you still wake up ready."

He didn't say for what. He didn't need to. She'd been always ready for anything with him, on waking up in his arms. Even now, when her mind wanted only to roast him slowly over an open fire, her body obeyed his inexorable influence, readying itself with a languid throb of remembrance and yearning.

And that was before his voice dropped another octave as he whispered, "If I woke you up, I'm glad. I shouldn't be the only one who can't sleep tonight."

"Your conscience weighing on you?" Her voice, to her dismay, was rough and thick, aroused, nowhere as demolishing as she intended it to be. "Or have you long had that removed? Or has it always been genetically missing?"

His chuckle was louder this time, more enervating. "Its deployment hasn't been required in our current situation. As I mentioned before, my offer is beneficial to everyone, starting with you. Now enough of that. What did you decide?"

"You mean I *can* decide? Now, that's a new development."

"It's a few-hours-old one. I already made it unquestionable that it's up to you. I just couldn't wait till morning for your verdict."

"Good thing that you called, so *I* wouldn't have to wait to tell you that I never want to see or hear from you again."

"That's not on the menu of options open to you. Being my temporary princess is a done deal. And as such, you'll see plenty of me. I'm only inquiring if you've decided to see *all* of me."

Her huff was less exasperated with him than disgusted with the clench of longing at his lazy, overpowering seduction. "I guess you decided to develop a sense of humor and you had to start from scratch. I must have your late blooming to thank for this juvenile double-talk."

"I apologize for my trite attempts at euphemisms." He sounded serious all of a sudden. Just as she wondered if she'd finally managed to offend him, his voice plunged into the darkest reaches of temptation. "So when will you let me strip you naked, worship and own and exploit every inch of your mind-blowing new curves for my pleasure and yours? When will you let me kiss and caress you within an inch of your sanity, suckle and stroke you to a few screaming orgasms before sinking inside you and riding you into oblivion?"

Breath sheared out of her lungs, heartbeats fractured against her ribs. The surge of images crowded her mind's eye with memories of her desperation for his touch and assuagement.

She'd asked for that when she'd taunted him. Not that she'd thought he'd say...

"Mind-blowing new curves?"

She almost groaned. She couldn't believe that was what she'd latched on to in all the mind-melting things he'd just said. Seemed body-image issues were so hardwired that they'd override even the heart attack he'd almost given her. But she *had* put on weight she wasn't happy about and couldn't believe he found it appealing.

"Ah, *si, bellissima,* every inch of you has...appreciated.

You were always gorgeous down to your toes, but the years have ripened you into something impossibly…more. I ached the whole time you were at my penthouse to test and taste every remembered wonder, every new enhancement. I am now in agony to explore and devour every part of you. And I know you need every part of me, too, on you, in you. I can feel your arousal echoing mine even at this distance. But if you think you're not ready yet, I'll come…persuade you. I'll remind you what it was like between us, prove to you how much better it will be now we're both older and wiser and certain of what we want."

Fighting another surge of response and haywire heartbeats, she said, "Now that I'm older and wiser, you think I'll let you have me without guarantees, like when I was young and stupid?"

"You want a ring first? I can bring it with me right now."

"*No.* That's not what I meant…." She gulped, her head spinning. This was zooming beyond warp speed. Just a few hours ago she'd never thought she'd see him again. Now he was almost seducing her, over the phone no less, and she was a breath away from telling him to just hurry the hell over. "I didn't mean material guarantees. I meant guarantees of being treated with respect when you decide I'm no longer 'convenient.' I don't even have the advantage or excuse of obliviousness like I did when I believed you valued me."

A silent moment followed. Then an expressionless drawl. "Let's leave the past buried. We're different people now."

"Are we? Maybe you are, whatever the hell you are. But unlike you, I have one basic character, and I'm pretty much the same person I was six years ago. Just older and wiser, as you pointed out, and aware that what you're suggesting would cause long-term damage. And mentioning that, if I become your 'princess,' temporary or not…"

"*When* you become my princess. Very soon. Though, with

the necessary preparations, not soon enough. But say the word, and I'll be worshiping your glorious body within the hour—"

She cut him off before she combusted. "I demand to have a say in the details, since I have no choice in the fundamental stuff. If part of this charade is a ring, then I want to choose it. You'll have it back in the end, but I'm the one who's going to be wearing it, and 'only a year' is still a long time."

His voice suddenly lost the mind-scrambling sexiness and filled with a different passion. "Then you will choose your ring. And everything else you want. As my princess you can and will have everything you wish for."

Her heart squeezed into her throat. "Weird. I have a two-hundred-page volume detailing how I can't have anything."

Silence stretched over long seconds.

A forcible exhalation followed. "That volume is only to…" He stopped again. As if he couldn't find the right words. Which was even weirder. Vincenzo was never at a loss for words.

She decided to help him out. "Only to protect you from any opportunistic ideas I might develop at contract termination. So it's strange you're willing to be wide-open for those same ideas at its start. Not that I want anything from you, but I'm just observing the contradictions."

Another long silence answered her.

Then another heavy exhalation. "I changed my mind."

He did? He was taking back his offer of "everything"? Figured. That must have been his need to have sex talking. She must have managed to douse his desire and he was back to thinking straight, and taking back his reckless concessions.

Then he went on. "You don't have to sign if you find it excessive. And you don't have to make a decision now. And you *are* free to say no. Of course, I won't stop trying to persuade you. But for now, you can go back to sleep. I'll come for you tomorrow at five to pick the ring. Sorry if I woke you up."

The line went dead.

She pulled the phone from her ear, staring down at it.

What was that all about? Had that been a fourth man inhabiting his body?

What was she walking into? And with which man? Or would it be with all of them? With him changing from one to the other until he drove her mad with confusion, insane with wanting him—whoever he was—and self-destructing in the process?

Not that she had any choice. She'd enter his den, and wouldn't exit it for the next year. It was doubtful she'd exit in one piece.

No. Not doubtful.

Impossible.

Four

"Impossible!"

Vincenzo cocked his head at his valet's stupefaction. The fondness Alonzo always stirred in him relaxed lips that had been spastic with tension since his conversation with Glory last night.

Even over the phone, she'd seeped under his skin and into his system and confounded his common sense. He shouldn't have called her in the first place. But he'd been unable to stop. The indiscretion alone had been enough to expose his condition, but he hadn't left anything to her imagination, had told her in exhaustive detail he was burning for her.

Then at the first tinge of disappointment and indignation in her voice, he'd offered anything at all in hope of erasing it. He'd taken back every precaution his mind—not to mention his attorney—insisted were indispensable to protect him.

He jerked back to the moment as Alonzo, in a totally uncharacteristic action, grabbed him by the shoulders.

"Are you teasing me? Because I was lamenting the other day that it seemed both of us would end up shriveled-up bachelors? But…you never joke." Alonzo's vivid green eyes widened. "*Dio.* You mean it. You *are* getting married."

He hadn't told Alonzo why, or how. For reasons he wasn't up to facing, he wanted Alonzo to think this was real. And to treat the whole thing accordingly. To treat Glory accordingly.

"When? *How?*" Alonzo grabbed his own head in dramatic disbelief. "You met a woman, fell in love with her, decided to marry her, asked her and had her agree without my knowledge?"

That would have been an impossibility, indeed. Alonzo was almost his shadow, had been indispensable to him since his teens, even before he lost his parents, smoothing out his daily life, anticipating his needs and providing him with hassle-free, meticulous support and problem solving in everything that didn't involve work and most things that did. He'd only gotten Glory's visit under Alonzo's radar because he'd sent him on some needless errand. Not that Alonzo would have recognized her. In a weird coincidence, Alonzo had taken his one and only prolonged leave of absence during Vincenzo's affair with Glory. It was probably the reason she'd been able to breach him that totally….

Oh, who was he fooling? He'd been the one and only reason. He'd left himself wide-open to her. And as she'd shrewdly commented, he was doing it again.

Clearly unaware of his turmoil, Alonzo pursued his own perplexity. "But most important, who?" Alonzo grimaced as if at an unsavory thought. "Please, don't tell me it's one of those women you parade for the paparazzi!"

This was another of the privacies that only Alonzo was privy to. That Vincenzo's reputation had been manufactured. By him. To keep hopeful and gold-digging women away. To keep women away, period. He'd found a ruthless playboy's image much more effectively off-putting than a reclusive scientist-prince's. Around a year after breaking up with Glory, he'd started hiring "escorts" wherever he went, to paint the image he wanted.

Not that he hadn't been with women outside his propaganda campaign. He'd tried. If not for long. After a few encounters had ended with him being unable to...rise to the occasion, he'd given up. Alonzo had even once asked if Vincenzo had changed his mind about his orientation, asking if he could take the glad tidings to the gay community that Vincenzo might be on the market soon.

Alonzo had been scandalized when Vincenzo had told him he'd just decided to take an open-ended leave of absence from sex. According to Alonzo, that was the most unnatural thing he'd ever heard. A virile man in his prime owed it to the world to give and receive pleasure to and from as many people as possible. Since he had no partner, of course.

But that had been the problem. While Vincenzo didn't have a partner, his body didn't know that. It had already been imprinted with Glory's code. And though his mind had rejected her, there'd been no reprogramming his body.

Now he decided to tell Alonzo what would appeal to the hopeless romantic in him. What had been true, if he didn't mention the parts that made it also ugly and painful.

"Her name is Glory Monaghan. She's an American who was once my executive consultant, and now she's consulting for major humanitarian operations. I fell in love with her during that time you went with Gio to Brazil. It ended...badly. Then Ferruccio slammed me with a royal decree to get married to clean up my image so I can be Castaldini's representative to the United Nations. And after all these years, and in spite of the way we parted, she was the only one I could think of. I sought her out again and found her hold on me is stronger than ever. Things...developed, and now...I'll marry her."

Alonzo's eyes, which had been reddening as he listened, now filled. "Oh, *mio ragazzo caro!* I have no words…no words…"

Vincenzo wondered if he'd ever get used to Alonzo calling him "dear boy." And he wondered if he was making a mistake by hiding the nature of his impending marriage.

Alonzo interrupted his heavy musings by doing something he hadn't done since Vincenzo was twelve. He pulled Vincenzo into a fatherly hug. Alonzo *had* been that to him, even more than his real father, though Bernardo D'Agostino had been an exceptional father, too.

Vincenzo accepted Alonzo's distraught joy, only wishing it was founded on something genuine, already starting to regret that he'd misled him.

Before he could make qualifications that would temper Alonzo's delight and expectations, and his subsequent letdown when things came to an inevitable end, Alonzo pulled back with a look of absolute anxiety on his face.

"Please tell me you're giving me enough time to prepare!"

Vincenzo shook his head, his lips once again tugging at how passionately Alonzo felt about everything. "Anyone hearing you would think it's your wedding, Alonzo."

"If only!" Alonzo's eyes filled with mockery and not a little resignation. "If Gio hasn't popped the question in fifteen years, he isn't about to do so now."

And for that, Vincenzo considered Giordano Mancini a major ass. Everyone knew Alonzo was his partner, but Giordano seemed to think that if he didn't openly admit it and didn't live with him he would avoid the prejudices that plagued same-sex relationships. As a businessman who came from a deeply traditional family, everyone turned a blind eye to his sexual orientation as long as he wasn't blatant about it.

Which outraged Vincenzo to no end. He considered Giordano a coward who shortchanged Alonzo to protect himself.

So same-sex marriages were still not accepted in Castaldini, but Vincenzo had told Gio he'd stand up for them, make sure everyone showed them every respect and courtesy, personally and professionally. His assurances hadn't been enough for Gio, and he'd convinced Alonzo that they didn't need a certificate or the world's acceptance to be happy. Or at least, Alonzo pretended to be convinced so he could stay with the man he loved. But his reaction now proved that he still yearned for the validation of his beloved's public proclamation, and the delight of preparing a ceremony to celebrate their bond.

Vincenzo's gaze settled heavily on Alonzo. Everyone thought Vincenzo couldn't be more different from the man, fourteen years his senior, who'd been his closest companion since he was ten. Only he knew how similar they were where it mattered. They were both detail-oriented and goal-focused. But most important, they suffered from the same fundamental ailment. Monogamy. The one thing stopping him from telling Alonzo to kick that guy out of his life was that Gio was equally exclusive.

At least so far. Vincenzo had made certain. If that ever changed, Gio wouldn't know what hit him.

"But it's worse." Alonzo's exclamation interrupted Vincenzo's aggressive thoughts. "It's *your* wedding. Do you know how long I've waited for this day?"

"I can subtract, Alonzo. Since you started droning that I should get married when I wasn't yet twenty. It's been two decades since you started longing to plan the elusive day."

"But it's elusive no more! I could kiss King Ferruccio for pushing you to make the decision."

"You just want to kiss Ferruccio under any pretext," he teased.

After that, Alonzo deluged him with questions, milking him for info on dates, preferences, Glory and everything besides, so he could start preparing the "Wedding of the Century," as he was adamant it would be. He insisted he'd have to get his hands on Glory ASAP so he'd get her input, and construct the perfect "setting" for Vincenzo's royal jewel.

Alonzo only left him alone when he told him of his ring-picking mission, for which he'd yet to prepare.

Alonzo almost skipped out of the room in his excitement about the million things he had to arrange and the prospect of his prince getting a princess at last.

Once alone, Vincenzo attacked planning the perfect ring rendezvous with as much single-mindedness as he did his most crucial scientific or business endeavors. But even with his far-reaching influence, it still took hours to prepare things to his satisfaction, leaving only two before his self-imposed appointment with Glory.

He rushed into his bathroom, ticking off the things he needed to do. To get ready for her.

Lust and longing seethed in his arteries as he entered the shower cubicle, letting the hot water sting some measure of relief into his tension. Not that it worked. He felt about to explode, as he had when he'd called Glory. He'd felt he might suffer some lasting damage if he didn't spend the rest of the night all over her, inside her, assuaging the hunger that had come crashing to the fore at renewed exposure to her.

But although he was still in agony, he was glad she'd resisted him, and that he'd backed off. And he was fiercely satisfied that his domineering tactics had made her push back. This was how he wanted it, wanted her, giving him the elation of the struggle, the exhilaration of the challenge. And she'd done that and more. She'd asked to pick her ring.

Suddenly, something that had been clenched inside him since he'd lost his dream of a life with her unfurled. The plan he'd started executing only twenty-four hours ago had been derailed. It had taken on a life of its own. He no longer had the least control over it or himself.

And he couldn't be more thrilled about it.

She's bewitched you all over again.

He smirked at that inner voice's effort to jolt him out of his intentions. It failed. He didn't care if she had. All his caution and self-preservation had only brought him melancholy and isolation. He was sick of them, of knowing that without her, he'd feel this way forever. It had taken seeing her again to prove that she was the only thing to bring him to life.

It might feel this way, but it's an illusion. It has always been.

He still didn't care. If the illusion felt that good, why not succumb to it? As long as he knew it was one.

What if knowing still won't protect you when it ends?

He frowned at the valid thought.

But no. Anything was better than the rut he was in. Apart from those months he'd had with her, all he'd done since he could remember was research, perform his business and royal duties, eat, exercise and sleep. Rinse and repeat in an unending cycle of emotional vacuum. Alone.

But when he had her again, he wouldn't be alone anymore. And he'd slake that obdurate sex drive of his with the only one who fueled and quenched it, who satisfied his every taste and need. For a year.

What if it isn't enough? What if you start this and sink so deep you can't climb out again? Last time you almost drowned. You barely survived, with permanent damage.

So be it. He was doing this. Letting go and gorging on every second of her. At whatever risk. He'd never have a real marriage, anyway. His only chance of that had been with her. Now that he'd already experienced the worst, he'd be prepared. At the end of the year, if he still wanted her as unstoppably as he did now, he'd negotiate an extension. And another, and another, until this unquenchable passion died out. It *had* to be extinguished at some point.

What if it only rages higher until it consumes you?
No, it wouldn't.
You're only hoping it won't. Against all evidence.
So what if it did consume him? After six barren years of safeguarding his emotions until they atrophied, of expanding his achievements until they'd swallowed up his existence, not to mention being bored out of his mind and dead inside, maybe it was time to live dangerously. Maybe being consumed wasn't such a bad idea. Or maybe it was, but so what?

He couldn't think of a better way to go.

And as long as he took her with him, he couldn't wait to hurl himself into the inferno.

Though she'd been counting down seconds, Glory's heart still rattled inside her rib cage like a coin inside an empty steel box when her bell rang at five o'clock sharp.

Smoothing hands damp with nervousness over the cool linen of her pants, she took measured steps to the door.

The moment she pulled the door open, she felt like she'd been hit by a car. And that was before she realized how Vincenzo looked. Exactly how he had looked the first time he'd shown up on her doorstep.

Her head spun, her senses stampeded with his effect now, with the reliving of his influence then.

A deepest navy silk suit, offset with a silver-gray shirt of the same spellbinding hue as his eyes, hugged the perfection of his juggernaut body. The thick waves of his hair were brushed back to curl behind his ears and caress his collar, exposing his virile hairline and leonine forehead. He even smelled of that same unique scent. Pine bodywash, cool seabreeze aftershave, fresh minty breath and the musk of his maleness and desire. His scent was so potent, she'd once believed it was an aphrodisiac. Her conviction was renewed.

Had he meant this? To show up on her doorstep like he

had that first day, only a minute after she'd said yes, making her realize he'd been already there? Dressed and groomed exactly like he had been then? The only difference was the maturity that amplified his beauty.

But there was another difference. In his vibe. His glance. His smile. A recklessness. A promise that there would be no rules and no limits.

Vincenzo? The man who had more rules and limits than his scientific experiments and developments? The prince who was forcing her to marry him to abide by his kingdom's social mores?

Maybe her perception was on the fritz. Which made sense. Vincenzo had always managed to blow her fuses. In spite of everything, all she wanted now was to drag him inside and lose herself in his greed and possession, have him reclaim her from the wasteland he'd cast her into, devour her, finish her...

"*Ringrazia Dio* for that way you look at me, *bellissima*...." He walked her back until he had her plastered against the wall. The sunlight slanting into her tiny but cheery foyer dimmed as his breadth blocked out the sun, the world. His aura enveloped her, his hunger penetrating her recesses, yanking at her. "As if you're starving for a taste of me. It would have been excruciating being the only one feeling this way."

Exactly what he'd said to her that first time.

He *was* reenacting that day.

That...that...*bastard!* What was he playing at?

Fury jerked her back from her sensuous stupor, infusing her backbone and voice with steel as she glared up at him. "You would have saved yourself the trip if you'd read my messages."

His hand moved, making her tense all over. His lips tugged as he touched her hair, smoothing it away from her cheek until she almost snatched his hand and pressed it against her flesh.

Then he made the feeling worse, bending to flay her with

his breath and words. "Oh, I read them. And chose to ignore them."

"Your loss." She almost gasped. "Their contents stand, whether you sanction them or not. I'm not going anywhere with you. Just give me whatever ring you have."

He withdrew to pour a devouring look down on her. "I would have gotten one if you'd said yes early this morning."

"Fine. When you get one, send it with one of your lackeys. And email instructions when you require I start advertising your image-cleansing campaign and wearing your 'brand.'"

His gaze melted her on its way down her body, taking in her casual powder-blue top and faded jeans, appreciation coloring the hunger there. "I see you believe you won't go out with me as you're not dressed for the occasion."

"There is no occasion, so I'm dressed in what suits a night at home. Alone."

This time, when his hand moved, it made contact with her flesh. A gossamer sweep with the back of his fingers down her almost combusting cheek. "You need to know that there are column A matters that are not open for negotiation. And then there are column B ones, where we either negotiate, or you can have whatever you like. Picking your ring is smack dab in column A."

Struggling so she wouldn't sink her teeth in his hand before dragging it to her aching breasts, she said, "Wow. You can even make a supposedly gallant gesture coercion."

"And reneging on our agreement is passive aggression."

"What agreement? You mean my stunned silence at your audacity in making an appointment without asking if I'm free?"

His pout was the essence of dismissal. "You're on vacation. I checked."

"I have a life outside of work. A personal life."

His self-satisfied grin made her palm itch for a stinging

connection with his chiseled cheek. "Not anymore. At least, none that doesn't involve me. Do get done with this tantrum so I can take you to pick your ring."

"It's you who's throwing a tantrum by insisting I pick it. Far from casting doubt on your impeccable taste when I asked to pick it, I was just trying to make a point, which I now see is pointless. I don't have any choice and pretending to have one in worthless stuff is just that—worthless. I've admitted it and moved on. So you don't have to prove your largesse by letting me grab a bigger rock, which is clearly what you think this is about."

All teasing evaporated from his eyes. "That didn't even cross my mind. I only want your taste not mine to dictate everything that will be intimate and personal to you."

"Wow. How considerate of you," she scoffed. "We both know you don't give a fig's peel about my opinion. And what intimate and personal things? This ring, and anything else you provide me with, is just a prop. What do I care what you deck me in? It's my role's costume and I'm returning everything at the end of this charade. And speaking of returning stuff, just so you're not worried I might 'lose' anything, or that you'll have to pay a steep premium on insuring it, just get me imitations. No one will dream anything you give me isn't genuine. And it would befit the fakeness of the whole setup."

The darkness on his face suddenly lifted. His eyes and lips resumed their provocation. "I must have been speaking Italian when I said this is nonnegotiable. Must be why we're having this breakdown in communications."

"Since I speak decent Italian—" she ignored his rising eyebrows; she wasn't telling him how and why she did "—it wouldn't have mattered which language you used. No is still my answer. It's the same in both languages."

His contemplation was now smoky, sensuous. "No is unacceptable. Are you prodding me into…persuading you?"

Knowing what kind of persuasion he'd expose her to, she slipped past the barrier of his bulk and temptation, staggered to her foyer's decorative storage cabinet and picked up the prenup. Her hands trembled as she turned and extended it to him.

He took it only when she thrust it against his chest, didn't even look at it, instead staring at her in that incapacitating way of his, his eyes like twin cloudy skies.

"I signed." Her voice was too breathless for her liking.

"I gave it to you to read. Signing would have been in duplicates, with both our legal counsels present."

She shrugged, confused at the note of disapproval—or was it disappointment?—in his voice. "Send me your copy to sign."

His gaze grew ponderous, probing. "Does that mean you didn't find it excessive?"

She huffed bitterly. "You know your Terms of Submission leave *excessive* in another galaxy. You only stop short of making provisions that I turn over the tan I acquire during my time in Castaldini."

"Then why did you sign? Why didn't you ask for changes?"

"You said it was nonnegotiable."

"I thought you'd have your attorney look at it, who'd tell you there's nothing in the world that isn't negotiable. I expected an alphabetized list of deletions and adjustments."

"I don't want any. I don't want *anything* from you. I never did. If you thought I'd haggle over your paranoid terms out of indignation or challenge or whatever, then you know nothing about me. But I already know that. You didn't consider me worth knowing, and I don't expect you to start treating me with any consideration now, when I'm just your smokescreen. So no, I don't care how far you go to protect yourself. This is what I want, too. It makes sure I'm out of your life, with no lingering ties whatsoever, the second the year is up."

Silence crashed in the wake of her ragged words.

Then he drawled, deep and dark, "A year is a long time."

Her pent-up breath rushed out. "Tell me about it. I just want to start serving my sentence with as little resistance as possible, so it will pass with as little damage as possible."

This time his gaze seemed to drill into her, as if to plumb the depths of her thoughts and emotions.

And she felt that he *could* read and sense everything she was thinking and feeling. Which was another new thing.

In the past, she'd always felt this…disconnection, except in the throes of passion. He'd been the classic absent-minded scientist, with his research occupying his fundamental being, only his superficial components engaged in everything else. Now it felt as if his whole being was tuned in to her. And that only deepened her confusion. What was he after?

Just as she tried to activate a two-way frequency to read him, he turned away, laying the prenup on her cabinet before turning back to her in utmost grace and tranquility.

"I'll wait while you put on something suitable for this momentous occasion. Any more stalling and I'll do it myself. I probably should since it's for my pleasure. I can also undress you first, for *our* pleasure. I remember in vivid detail how you used to enjoy both activities."

The avid look in his eyes said he'd carry out his silky threat at the slightest resistance. She couldn't risk it, since she might end up begging him not to stop at undressing her.

Exasperated with both of them in equal measure, her glare told him what would give her utmost pleasure now. Giving his perfect nose some crooked character.

Mumbling abuse, she stormed to her room, with his laughter at her back, sending her temperature into the danger zone.

Half an hour later, when loitering drove *her* to screaming pitch, she exited her room. She found him prowling her living area like a caged panther.

He stopped in midstep, taking in her new outfit. Or her old

one. The cream skirt suit with a satin turquoise blouse was...
adequate. Even with stilettos and a purse coordinating with
her blouse, it was nowhere near glamorous. But it was the only
outfit she'd kept from her corporate days. Her wardrobe now
consisted of a minimum of utilitarian clothes. Otherwise she
would have never picked this suit. It was what she'd worn to
her job interview with him. What she'd gone out with him in
when he'd insisted on not wasting time changing. Fate was
conspiring for her to take part in his déjà vu scenario.

She couldn't tell if he remembered the suit, since that devouring look he'd had since they'd met again remained un-
changed.

Before he could say anything, she preempted him. "In
case you find this lacking, too, tough. This is my one and
only 'momentous occasion' outfit. You're welcome to check."

"It is a 'momentous occasion' outfit indeed. If only for
being...nostalgic of one." So he remembered. Figured. He
had a computer-like mind. Their time together must be ar-
chived in one of his extensive memory banks. "But we must
do something about your wardrobe deficiencies. Your incomparable body must be clothed in only the finest creations. The
masters of the fashion world will fall over each other for the
chance to have your unique beauty grace theirs."

She just had to snort. "Uh...have you been diagnosed
with multiple personality disorder yet? Incomparable body?
Unique beauty? What do you call the persona that thinks
that?"

He started eliminating the distance between them, intent
radiating from him. "If I never told you how I find you breathtaking down to your pores, I need to be punished. Which you
are welcome to do. In my defense, I was busy showing you."

"Yeah, before you showed me the door, and told me how
interchangeable you found me with any female who wasn't
too hideous but meek and willing enough."

"I lied."

His gaze was direct, his words clear, cutting.

Disorientation rolled over her. "You—you did?"

His nod was terse, unequivocal. "Through my teeth."

"Why?"

His lids squeezed, before he opened them, his gaze opaque. "I don't want to go into the reasons. But nothing I said had any basis in truth. Let's leave it at that."

"And to hell with what *I* want. But then, you're getting what you want no matter what I desire or what it costs me. Why do I keep expecting anything different? I must be insane."

He seemed to hold back something impulsive. An elaboration on his cryptic declarations?

But she *needed* something. *Anything*. If what he'd said to her, the words that had torn into her psyche like shrapnel all those years ago, had all been lies, why had he said them? To push her away? Had she been clinging so hard that he'd panicked…?

No. She wasn't rationalizing that son of a bitch's mistreatment. There was no excuse for what he'd done to her. And now he was doing worse. Reeling her closer even as he pushed her away. Confounding her then leaving her hanging. Depriving her of the stability of hating him, the certainty of why she did.

His eyes were blank as he took her coat from her spastic grip, disregarding her bitterness. "We'll have dinner first."

She sullenly let him help her on with her coat, moving away as his arms started to tighten around her. "You're not worried about putting cutlery in my reach?"

His gaze melted with an indulgence that hurt and confused her more than anything else. "I'll take my chances."

"You really expect me to eat after…all this?"

"I'll postpone serving dinner until you're very hungry. By

then, I also hope your appetite for food will overpower that of poking me in the eye with a fork."

With a look that said fat chance, she preceded him out of her condo.

She ignored him as he tried to hand her into the front passenger seat of a gemlike burgundy Jaguar he had parked in her building's garage. He gave up acting the gallant suitor and walked around to take the wheel.

So. No driver, no guards. He wasn't making their liaison public yet. Because he hadn't expected her to sign the prenup, hadn't considered it a done deal? No doubt he'd planned to coerce her some more during this "momentous occasion" until she did. She wondered what recalculation was going on inside that inscrutable mind now that she'd made further manipulation unnecessary.

During the drive, she sat barely breathing or moving so his scent and presence wouldn't scramble her senses even more. Then observations finally seeped into her hazy mind.

They were leaving the city.

When she was certain this was no roundabout way to any restaurant or jeweler, she forced herself to turn to him.

"Where are we going?"

Still presenting her with the perfection of his profile, he smiled. "To the airport."

Five

"The airport?"

At her croak, Vincenzo's smile widened. "We're going to have dinner on the jet. We'll fly to where the most exclusive collection of jewelry on the planet awaits you, so you can pick your ring, and anything else that catches your fancy."

He was so pleased with himself for stunning her again.

She was more than stunned. She was working on a stroke.

"And it didn't occur to you to ask if I'd agree to this hare-brained scheme of yours?"

His lips twitched at her venom. "A man going out of his way to surprise his fiancée doesn't tell her in advance of the details of his efforts."

Her jaw muscles hurt at his mention of *fiancée*. "Do save your 'efforts' for when you have a real fiancée."

"But you already said I can't have a real one for all the money and power in the world."

"Who knows? Lots of women have self-destructive tendencies. And I didn't say you couldn't get one, I said you wouldn't keep her."

His eyes twinkled with mischief before he turned onto a route she'd never seen into the airport, and she'd been here countless times. "Well, you're real enough for me. And for as long as I keep you, I get to go all-out to surprise you."

She harrumphed. "Save your energy. And save me from a stroke. I hate surprises. I haven't met one that wasn't nasty. Certainly never any from you."

He sighed. "I assure you, this trip is anything but."

"I don't care what it will be like. It's the concept I can't stand." She exhaled exasperatedly. "And to think I once thought you were part bulldozer."

He slowed down as he took a turn, his eyebrows rising in amused query. "You changed your mind?"

"Yes. You're the pure breed."

And he did something that almost made her head explode. He threw *his* head back and let out a hearty guffaw.

When she felt he'd scrambled her nervous system forever, he turned to her, chuckles still reverberating deep in his end-less chest, his smile wider than she'd ever seen it.

"Watch it with the laughter, Vincenzo," she mumbled, hat-ing it that he affected her to extremes no matter what he was doing. "Doing something so unnatural to you can be danger-ous. You'll dislocate a brain lobe or something."

His laugh boomed again. "*Dio,* I can get used to this."

"Your highness hasn't been exposed to sarcasm before? Figures, with all the syrupy ass-kissing you have everywhere you turn. Since you've been exposed to it from birth, you must have always had social juvenile diabetes."

"I was wrong. I'm already too used to getting lashed with your delightful tongue. I hope you won't ever hold it."

"I think it's a physical impossibility with you around."

He chuckled again, this time doing something even more

distressing. He reached out for her hand and brought it to his lips.

His lips. Those lips that had enslaved her with their possession, that had taught her passion and the pleasure her body was capable of experiencing. The moment they touched the back of her hand, her heart almost ruptured.

She snatched her hand back as if from open fire, agitation searing her insides. "I don't know what you're playing at…"

"I already told you my game plan." His eyes turned serious as he brought the car to a stop and turned to her. "But I've also come to a new decision. I no longer care how this started…"

"I do."

"…I only care that when I'm with you I feel…great. I haven't felt like that in… I don't even remember if I ever felt like that. You invigorate me. Your every word and look thrills me, and I don't intend to keep holding back and not show it. If you tickle my humor, and you do, constantly, I'll laugh. And I want you to do the same. Forget how we got to be here…"

"Because you blackmailed me."

"…and just make the best of it. If you enjoy my company…"

"I'm not a fan of Stockholm syndrome, thank you."

"…just allow yourself the enjoyment, don't stifle it and don't keep telling yourself why you should hold it back."

"Easy for you to say and do. You're not the one being threatened with your family's imprisonment and taken hostage for a year. *And* being kidnapped right now."

His eyes grew coaxing. "You are my partner in an endeavor I'm undertaking to serve my kingdom." The word *partner,* the term he'd once said would never apply to her, scratched like a talon against her heart. "You will help me bridge its distance from the world to benefit its people and the coming generations. And you're the fiancée I'm taking on a surprise trip. I will do everything in my power so you will enjoy it."

The wish that all that could be true overwhelmed her, closing her throat. "That's the facade hiding the ugly truth."

"It *is* the truth, if you don't dwell on the negative aspects."

"Negative aspects? Now, that's an innovative euphemism for *extortion*."

He didn't segue into a rejoinder this time. His gaze lengthened, grew distant, as if he was looking inward.

Seeming to come back to her, he exhaled. "Would you marry me if I took your family out of the equation?"

It was her turn to stare. "You mean I can say no and you wouldn't report them?"

"Yes."

He looked and sounded serious. Yeah. Sure.

"I don't believe you."

"Understandable. I don't believe myself, either." His head-shake was self-deprecation itself. "But I do mean it."

"Is this a ploy to put me at ease? So I'll stop giving you a much deserved, not to mention much needed, hard time? So I'll stop resisting and 'come to your bed'?"

"Yes. No. Definitely." At her frown, he elaborated. "Yes, I want to put you at ease, though it's not a ploy. No, I don't want you to stop bashing me on the head. With the way I'm relishing it, I'm realizing how much I do need it. And I'm definitely anticipating you in my bed...." His arm snaked around her, pulled her into his heat and hardness, enervating her with the delight of his feel and scent. "I'm willing to do whatever it takes to have you racing me there as you used to."

Her head fell back as she stared at him, sounding as faint as she felt. "Even if it means not using your winning hand?"

"I already said it had nothing to do with our intimacies."

"How can I be sure you won't hurt my family if I say no?"

"How were you sure I wouldn't after you said yes? I guess you'll have to trust me."

"I don't." She'd trusted him before. Look where it had gotten her.

"We're even, then."

What? What did that mean?

Before she could voice her puzzlement, he pressed her harder, cupped her face, and her questions combusted at the feel of the warm, powerful flesh cradling hers. "Don't say anything now. Let's forget everything and go with the flow. Let me give us tonight."

Tonight. The word reverberated between them, sweeping through her, uprooting the tethers of her resolve and aversion. His lips were half a breath away, filling her lungs with his intoxication.

She hated that she yearned for his taste and urgency and dominance, but she did. How she did. The need screwed tighter, squeezing her vitals, strangling them. Everything that would assuage the craving gnawing her hollow was a tug away, on his lapel, his hair. Then he would give her everything she needed.

But she couldn't do it. Literally. She couldn't move a muscle. And he was giving her the choice of the first move. He wouldn't take that out of her hands, too. When that was where she needed him to leave her no choice.

Leave it to him to do the opposite of what she wanted.

Annoyance spurted, infusing her limpness with tension.

With a look acknowledging that he wouldn't get a cease-fire that easily, and with a last annihilating stroke across her stinging lips, he pulled back.

In moments he'd stepped down from the car and come around to her door. She almost clung to him for support as he handed her down. The coolness of twilight after the warmth of the vehicle sprouted goose bumps all over her, adding to her imbalance.

Then every concern evaporated as she gaped. Up.

They were beneath a massive jetliner that looked like a giant alien bird of prey. This was his jet?

The next moment left no doubt as he took her elbow and led her to the Air Force One–style stairs that led from the tarmac to the inside of the jet.

Once inside, her jaw dropped further. She'd been on private jets before, though never his. Another proof of how marginal she'd been to him, when he'd been the center of her universe. But any other jets she'd seen paled in comparison.

She turned sarcastic eyes up to him. "It's clear you believe in going the extra hundred million in pursuit of luxury."

He smiled down at her. "I wouldn't say I go that far."

She looked pointedly around. "I'd say you go beyond."

His smile remained unrepentant. "I travel a lot, with staff. I have meetings on board. I need space and convenience."

"Tell me about your need for those." She waited until she got a "so we won't stop dredging up the past, eh?" look, then added more derision. "And you must have yet another castle in the sky to accommodate both 'needs,' huh?"

"My family's being the first one on terra firma?"

"And the third being the futuristic headquarters in New York. Next, I'll find out you have a space station and a couple of pyramids. Hang on…"

She got out her phone.

He gave her a playful tug, plastering her to his side. "What are you doing now?"

Squeezing her legs tighter against the new rush of heat, she cocked her head up at him. "Just estimating how many thousands of children this sickeningly blatant status symbol could feed, clothe and educate for years."

He tipped his head back and his laughter boomed, sending her heartbeats scattering all over the jet's lush carpeting.

"*Dio,* will I ever come close to guessing what you'll say next?" He still chuckled as he led her through a meeting area, where staff hovered in the background, to the spiral staircase leading to the upper deck. "So you consider this jet too pretentious? A waste of money better spent on worthy causes?"

"Any personal 'item' with a price tag the length of a phone number ranges from ludicrously to criminally wasteful."

"Even if it's a utility that I use to make millions of dollars more, money I do use to benefit humanity at large?"

"By advancing science, protecting the environment and creating jobs? Yeah. You forget how I started my working life. I've heard all the arguments. And seen all the tax write-offs."

"But you started your working life with me, so you know I'm not in this to make money or to flaunt my power or status."

"Do I? Solid experience has taught me that I know nothing about the real you."

He didn't answer that as he walked her across an ultrachic foyer and through a door that he opened via a fingerprint-recognition module. It whirred shut as he let her lead him into what had to be the ultimate in airborne private quarters.

The sheer opulence hit her with more evidence of the world he existed in. The world he now maintained she could choose to enter, or not.

He guided her to one of the tan leather couches by huge oval windows and tugged her down with him. She hit the soft surface and it shifted to accommodate her body in the plushest medium she'd ever sat on. Not that she could enjoy the sensation with his body touching hers, making her feel split down the middle, with the half touching him burning and the other half freezing.

She tried to ignore him and her rioting senses by looking

around the grand lounge drenched in golden lights, earth tones and the serenity of sumptuousness and seclusion. At the far end of the huge space that spanned the breadth of the jet, a wall was decorated in intricate designs from the blend of cultures that made up Castaldini: Roman, Andalusian and Moorish. A double door led to another area. No doubt a bedroom suite.

A ghost of a touch zapped through her like a thousand volts. His finger feathering against her face, turning it to his.

"Regarding the 'real me,' as you put it," he said, his eyes simmering in the golden lighting. "If you insist you don't know him, let me rectify this." He sank deeper into the couch, taking her with him until their heads leaned on the headrest, their faces close enough for her to get lost in the pattern of his incredible irises. "The real me is a nerd who happens to have been born in a royal family then inherited lots of money. He owes not squandering said fortune on his research and impractical ideas to the teachers he's been blessed with, who tutored him in business practices, and directed his research and resources into money-making products and facilities. He, alas, never had the temperament or desire to become a corporate mogul."

"Yet 'he' became one, and as ruthless as they come." To her chagrin, her denunciation sounded like a cooing endearment.

"'He' basically found himself one. And I must contest the ruthless part. Though 'he' makes too much money, it's not by adopting cold-blooded bottom-line practices. It just happens that the methods those people taught him are that efficient."

Her own fundamental fairness got the best of her. "No one could have helped you make a cent, let alone such a sustained downpour, if you hadn't come up with something so ingeniously applicable and universally useful."

"And I wouldn't have gotten any of that translated into reality without those people."

Her heart hammered at his earnest words. At the memories they exhumed.

She'd once poured all her time and effort into providing him with a comprehensive plan for his future operations. He'd already had an exceptional head for business when he applied his off-the-charts IQ to it, but it hadn't been his specialty or his focus. And he *had* had some unrealistic views and expectations when it came to translating his science into practice. So she'd insisted on educating him in what would come after the breakthrough, how his R&D and manufacturing departments would sync and work at escalating efficiency and productivity to streamline operations and maximize profit.

That had been another of the injustices he'd dealt her as he'd discarded her, evaluating her only based on her sexual role, as if she'd never offered him anything else. That had cut deeper into her the more she'd dwelled on it. It had taken her a long time to recover her sense of self-worth.

She bet he didn't count her among those teachers fate had blessed him with.

A finger ran gently down her cheek. "You're at the top of the list of those people."

She blinked. He admitted that?

"I owe you for most of the bad decisions I didn't make before the good ones I did make."

Her heart stumbled, no longer knowing how hard or fast to beat, thoughts and emotions yo-yoing so hard she felt dizzy.

She shook her head as if to stop the fluctuations. "Is this admission part of your efforts to 'put me at ease'?"

"It's the truth."

"Not according to you six years ago. Or forty-eight hours ago."

His eyes misted with something like melancholy. "It's not the whole truth, granted." Now, what did *that* mean? "But I'm sick and tired of pretending this didn't happen, that there were no good parts. There were…incredible parts. And no matter why you offered me this guidance, you did offer it, and I did use it to my best advantage, so…*grazie mille, bellissima.*"

This time she gaped at him for what felt like an hour.

What did this confounding man want to do to her? Was he truly suffering from a multiple personality disorder? What else could explain his contradictions?

But he'd already said he wouldn't explain. So there was no use pursuing it.

Deciding not to give him the satisfaction of a response to his too-late, too-little thanks, she cast a look around. "I still think this level of luxury is criminal."

His smile dawned again, incinerating all in its path. "Sorry to shoot down your censure missiles, but this isn't my jet. It's the Castaldinian Air Force One." So her earlier observation was true! "Ferruccio put it at my disposal as soon as I told him of you, in his efforts to see me hitched…ASAP."

As he grinned as if at a private joke, something inside her snapped.

She whacked him on the arm, hard.

His eyebrows shot up in surprise that became hilarity, and then he was letting out peal after peal of laughter.

"Had your joke at my expense?" she seethed.

"I was actually basking in your abuse," he spluttered.

"Why didn't you say you developed masochistic tendencies in your old age? You don't need to manipulate me into obliging your perversion. The desire to shower abuse on your unfeeling head is my default setting." She'd bet her glare would have withered rock. That hunk of unfeeling male perfection only chuckled harder. She attempted a harder verbal volley. "That this jet isn't yours doesn't exonerate you. You probably have your own squadron that puts it to shame. But apparently you're so cheap you'd rather use state property and funds."

"Damned if I do and if I don't, eh?" He didn't seem too

upset about it, but looked like she'd just praised him heartily as he picked up her hand and brought it to his lips. "Sheathe your claws, my azure-eyed lioness."

She gritted her teeth as his lips moved against her knuckles. "Why? Didn't you just discover that you relish being ripped to shreds?"

He sighed his enjoyment. "Indeed. But it works better when you're slamming me over my real flaws. Being pretentious and exploitative isn't among my excesses and failings. If you think so then you haven't kept abreast with my pursuits."

That made her snort. "You mean you think it's possible to avoid those? When your face and exploits are plastered everywhere I go? You even come out of the faucet when I turn it on. My building has turned to your services for heating."

His laugh cracked out again.

In spite of wanting to smack him again, that sense of fairness still prodded her to add, "But among all that obnoxious overexposure, I do know your corporations have substantial and varied aid programs."

That seemed to surprise him. "The world at large doesn't know about this side of my activities. I wonder how you knew."

Her smirk told him two could play at withholding answers. "It's I who wonders what you're after with all the discreet philanthropy. Are you playing at being Bruce Wayne? If you are, all that's left is for you to don the cape, mask and tights…" She paused as his laughter escalated again then mumbled, "Since making you feel great is nonexistent on my list of priorities, I'll shut up now."

He leaned closer until his lips brushed her temple. He didn't kiss her, just talked against her flesh. "I'd beg you not to. I don't think I can live now without being bombarded by the shrapnel that keeps flying out of your mouth."

She kept said mouth firmly closed.

To incite another salvo—she was sure—his lips moved to the top of her cheekbone, in the most languid, heart-melting kiss.

She jumped to her feet, nerves jangling.

He was somehow on his feet before her, blocking her way. "If you're not going to abuse me, how about you use your mouth for something else?" He waited until her chagrin seethed and blasted out of her in a searing glare before adding in provocative pseudo innocence, "Eat?"

"It's safer for you if I'm not near cutlery tonight."

"Nonsense. I'm not in the least worried. What's the worst you could do with disposable ones?"

This was beyond weird. Had he always had a sense of humor, but just hadn't turned it on in her presence? Why did he have it perpetually on now?

Giving up trying to understand this baffling entity, yet refusing to give him an answer, she turned away, headed to the lavatory. She needed a breather before the next round.

When she came out, she faltered, trying to breathe around a lump that materialized in her throat.

He'd taken off his jacket. And had undone a few buttons on his shirt. And rolled up his sleeves.

It probably wouldn't affect her any more if he'd taken off all his clothes. Okay, it would, but this was bad enough. The imagination that was intimate with his every inch was filling in the spaces, or rather, taking off the rest of his clothes.

He smiled that slow smile of his, no doubt noting the drool spreading at her feet. Then he extended that beautifully formed—and from experience, very talented—hand in invitation.

She covered the space between them as if by his will alone, unable to stop devouring his magnificence.

Reality again outstripped imagination or memory. The breadth and power of his shoulders and chest had owed nothing to tailoring. They were even magnified now that they were covered only in a layer of finest silk. His arms bulged with strength and symmetry under the material that obscured and highlighted at once. Those corded forearms dusted with black hair tapered to solid wrists. His abdomen was hard, his waist narrow, as were his hips, before his thighs flowed with strength and virility on the way down to endless legs.

Magnificent wasn't even a fitting description.

He sat back down on the couch, patting where he wanted her to sit. On his lap.

She wanted to. To just lose her mind all over him, let him seduce her, own her, drain her of will and blow her mind with pleasure, again and again and again, for as long as it took him to have enough of her this time, and to hell with caution and the lessons of harsh experience.

Before she decided to take a flying jump into the abyss, he engulfed her hand in the warm power of his and gave a tug that was persuasion and urgency itself. She tumbled over him, her skirt riding up as her thighs splayed to straddle him.

The moment she felt him against her, between her legs, the rock hardness and heat of his chest and his erection pressing against her breast and core, arousal surged so fiercely she almost fainted. Then his lips opened over her neck, and she did swoon, melting over him.

His hands convulsed in the depths of her hair, harnessing her for his devouring as his mouth took pulls of her flesh, as if he'd suck her heartbeats, her essence into him. Her head fell back, arching her neck, giving him fuller access, surrendering her wariness and heartache to his pleasuring.

She needed this, needed him, come what may.

"You feel and taste even better than all the memories that tormented me, *Gloria mia.*"

She jerked and moaned when he said her name the way he used to, Italianizing it, making it his. It inflamed her to hear it, maddened her. The way he moved against her, breathed her in, touched and kneaded and suckled her…it was all too much. And too little. She needed more. Everything. His mouth and hands and potency all over her, inside her.

"Vincenzo…"

The same desperation reverberating inside her emanated from his great body in shock waves. Then he heaved beneath her, swept her around, brought her under him on the couch, bore down on her with all of his greed and urgency. Spreading her thighs, he hooked them around his hips, pressed between them, his daunting hardness grinding against her entrance through their clothes. Her back arched deeply to accommodate him, a cry escaping from her very recesses, at the yearned-for feel of him, weight of him, sight of him as propped himself above her, his eyes molten steel with the vehemence of his passion.

"Gloriosa, divina, Gloria mia…"

Then he swooped down and his lips clamped on hers, moist, branding, his tongue thrusting deep, singeing her with pleasure, breaching her with need, draining her of moans and reason. Pressure built—behind her eyes, inside her chest, deep in her loins. Her hands convulsed on his arms, digging into his muscles, everything inside her surging, gushing, needing anything…anything he'd do to her. His fingers and tongue and teeth exploiting her every secret, his manhood filling the void at her core, thrusting her to oblivion….

"We'll be taking off in five minutes, *Principe*."

The voice rang in a metallic echo, not registering in the delirium. It was only when he stopped his plundering kisses that it crashed into her awareness, that it made sense.

He froze over her for a long moment, his lips still fused to hers. He moved again, took her lips over and over in urgent, clinging kisses as if he couldn't help himself, as if he was gulping what he could of her taste before he could have no more. Then muttering something savage under his breath, he severed their meld, groaning as if was scraping off his skin. It was how she felt, too, as his body separated from hers.

She lay back, stunned, unable to move. Dismay at the barely aborted insanity drenched her, even as need still hammered at her, demanding his assuagement. His heavy-lidded gaze regarded her in denuding intensity, as if savoring the sight of what he'd done to her. Then he reached for her, caressed and kneaded her as he helped her up on the couch.

He secured her seat belt before buckling his as the engines, which she realized had been on for a while now, revved higher and the jet started moving.

They were really taking off.

Everything was going out of control, too far, too fast.

And she had no idea where they were going. Figuratively and literally.

The latter had a definite answer. And in an existence that had no answers, past or future, she had to have at least that.

"Where are we going?"

At her unsteady question, he pulled her closer, his eyes blazing with unspent desire. "How about we keep it a surprise?"

"How about I go demand that your pilot drop me off?"

He tutted. "I see I have to surprise you with no warning next time."

"Since you can't take me somewhere without warning unless you develop teleportation, too…"

"Or kidnap you for real and keep you tied up and gagged on the way."

"…then get a *real* surprise when you finally untie and ungag me. Something broken or bitten off or both."

Looking even more aroused and elated, he gathered her tighter, put his lips to her ear, nipped her lobe and whispered, "We're going to Castaldini."

Six

Glory had one thought. That she wasn't going to repeat his words. No matter how flabbergasted she was that he'd said…

"Castaldini."

God. *No.* He was making her echo his declarations like a malfunctioning playback.

She pushed out of his arms, whacked him on both this time, as hard as she could.

"No, we're *not* going to Castaldini," she hissed.

He caught his lower lip in beautiful white teeth, wincing in evident enjoyment at her violence, rubbing the sting of her blow as if to drive it deeper, not away. "Why not?"

She barely held from whacking him again. "Because you conned me."

"I did no such thing."

"When you said we were flying, I assumed it would be to another city or at most another state."

"Am I responsible for your faulty assumptions? I gave

you all the clues, said I'm taking you where the most exclusive jewelry on the planet awaits you. Where did you think that was?"

"I didn't realize you were playing Trivial Pursuit at the time. And why go all this way for a ring? What's that hyperbole about Castaldinian jewelry? Is that exaggerated national pride where you claim everything in Castaldini is the best in history?"

"I don't know about everything, but I'm pretty sure Castaldini's royal jewels are as exclusive as it gets."

"Castaldini's royal j—" Her teeth clattered shut before she completed parroting this latest piece of astounding info. Shock surged back a moment later. "You can't be serious! I can't wear a ring from Castaldini's freaking royal jewels!"

"*You* can't be serious thinking my bride would wear anything else."

"I'm not your bride. I'm your decoy. And that only for a year. But as you said, a year can be a very long time. I can't take the responsibility for something that…that priceless…." She pushed his hands away when they attempted to draw her back into his embrace. "For God's sake, during the height of Castaldini's economic problems, before King Ferruccio was crowned, people were saying that if only Castaldini sold half of those jewels, they'd settle the national debt!"

"Oh, I did propose the solution. But Castaldinians would rather sell their firstborns."

"And you want me to wear a ring from a collection that revered, for any reason, let alone a charade? You expect me to walk around wearing a kingdom's legacy on my finger?"

"That's exactly what you'll do as my bride. In fact, you yourself will be a new national treasure. Now that's settled…"

"Nothing's settled," she spluttered, feeling she was in a whirlpool that dragged her deeper the more she struggled. "I won't go to Castaldini. Now tell your pilot to turn back."

A look came into his eyes that made her itch to hit him again. One of *such* patient reasonableness. "You knew you'd go to Castaldini sooner rather than later."

"I thought you said I could say no to your blackmail."

His nod was equanimity itself. "I said I wouldn't expose your family if you said no. But if you say yes, I'll make sure they will never be exposed."

Ice crept into her veins again. "Wh-what do you mean?"

"They've committed too many crimes. It's only a matter of time before someone finds out what I have. Marry me and I'll do everything in my power to wipe their trail clean."

"That's just another roundabout blackmail."

"Actually, it's the opposite. Before, I said I'd hurt them if you say no. Now I'm saying I'll help them if you say yes."

Her head spun, her thoughts tangling like a ball of twine after a wicked cat had gotten to it. He was the feline to her own cornered mouse.

"I don't see how that's different. And even if I say yes…"

He caught her hands, pressed them into the heat of his steel muscles. "Say it, *Gloria mia.* Give me your consent."

"Even if I do…"

"Do it. Say you'll be my bride."

She squirmed away from his intensity. "Okay, okay, yes. Dude, you're pushy."

He huffed mockingly. "Such eagerness. Such graciousness."

"If you think I owe you either, you're out of your zillion-IQ mind. And this doesn't mean anything's changed. Or that's it's not still under duress. It certainly doesn't mean I consent to going to Castaldini now."

He sat back, all tension leaving his body, a look of gratification sweeping across his breathtaking face. "Give me one reason why you're so against going."

She had to blink to clear the glaze of hypnosis from her eyes. "I can give you a volume as thick as your prenup."

"One incontestable reason should suffice. And 'because I don't want to' doesn't count."

"Of course what I want doesn't count. You made *that* clear."

His pout made her want to drag him down and sink her teeth into those lips that had just reinjected his addiction into her system. "I made it clear that I changed my mind, about many things. Be flexible and change yours."

"I don't owe you any flexibility, either. I let you steamroll me by letting me think this was going to be a short trip inside my country. I didn't sign on to leave it."

"As my bride, you will leave it. Though not forever."

"Yeah, only for a one-year term. But I get to choose when that will begin."

"I meant you'd always be free to return, to go anywhere. This time, you can go back to New York tomorrow if you wish."

"I don't want to leave New York in the first place. I can't just hop to another country!"

"Why not? You do that all the time in your work."

"Well, this isn't work. And speaking of work, I can't drop everything with no notice."

"You're on vacation, remember?"

"I have other things to do besides work."

"Like what?" He met her fury with utmost serenity.

"Okay, I changed my mind, too. You're not a bulldozer. You're an ocean. You'd erode mountains. No, a tsunami. You uproot everything, subside only with everything submerged under your control."

He chuckled. "As much as I enjoy having you dissect and detail my vices, food is becoming a pressing issue. I had the chef prepare favorite dishes from Castaldini for you to sample."

Her hands itched to tweak that dimpled cheek, hard. "Don't change the subject."

Ignoring her, he undid his seat belt, then leaned into her, undoing hers. "You really shouldn't risk me getting any hungrier—in every way."

Her gaze slid to the evidence of one hunger and...whoa.

She tore her gaze up, only to slam into his watchful, knowing, enticing one. Gasping with the need to explore him, she said, "Even in food you're giving me no choice."

He separated from her lingeringly, pushing buttons in a panel by the couch. It was still only when he stood up that she realized they were cruising steadily.

"I am. *My* choice is to feast on you and to hell with food. I'm giving you the choice to avoid what you really want by choosing food, for now."

She bit back a retort. It would be silly to deny his assessment, when only the pilot's announcement had saved her from being wrapped around him naked right now, begging for—and taking—everything.

Exasperated with both of them, she ignored his inviting hand to rise and walk to where he indicated. Behind a screen of gorgeous lacelike woodwork at the far end of the lounge by the closed quarters was a stunning table-for-two setup.

Though everything in the compartment felt like authentic masterpieces, with the distinctive designs of seventeenth- or eighteenth-century Castaldini, the furniture was discreetly mounted on rails embedded in the fuselage. Exquisite, delicately carved, polished mahogany chairs were upholstered in burgundy glossy-on-matte floral-patterned silk. The matching round table was draped in the most intricate beige tape-lace tablecloth she'd ever seen, set over longer burgundy organza, with its pattern echoing the stunning hand-painted china laid out on top. Lit candles, crystal glasses, a vase with a conflagration of burgundy and cream roses, linen napkins, silver cutlery and a dozen other accents—all monogrammed with the royal insignia of Castaldini—completed the breathtaking arrangement.

She looked up at him as he slid the chair back for her. "I somehow can't imagine King Ferruccio here."

His eyebrows rose as he sat across her. "You mean you still think it's my jet?"

It hadn't occurred to her to doubt that or anything else he'd said. She'd believed his every word, declaration and promise.

Which was only more proof that fools never, ever learned.

She sighed. "It's not that. The rest of the jet is so grand, befitting a king and then some. But *this* setting is too…"

"Intimate?" he chimed in when she made a stymied gesture around the dreamily lit space. "Your senses are on the money. This section was designed by Clarissa as her and Ferruccio's mile-high love nest."

Glory's simmering heat shot up, imagining all the pleasure that could be had here, and feeling she was intruding on someone's privacy. "You sure he's okay with you invading it?"

"He scanned my fingerprint into the controls."

"Let me put it this way, then. Are you sure he cleared it with Queen Clarissa?"

"What I'm sure of is if he didn't, he'd love to be punished for his unsanctioned actions."

Her lips twitched as she imagined the regal figure of King Ferruccio being spanked by his fair queen. "Another D'Agostino with a fetish for female abuse?"

"Ferruccio would let Clarissa step dance all over him and beg for more. But since she's part angel, she doesn't take advantage of his submissive affliction where she's concerned."

His expression softened as he talked about his queen and cousin. Though she'd been a princess first, the previous king's daughter, not much had been known about Clarissa before she became the illegitimate king's queen. Ever since their marriage, she'd become one of the most romantic royal figures in history. Glory had heard only great things about her.

It still twisted her gut to feel Vincenzo's deep fondness for the woman, to witness evidence that he was capable of such tender affections. What he hadn't felt for her. What she hadn't aroused in him.

Oblivious to her sudden plunge in mood, he smiled. "And speaking of access…"

He pushed a button on a panel by the huge oval window to his side. The door of the lounge whispered open. In moments, half a dozen waiters dressed in burgundy-and-black uniforms, with the royal emblem embroidered on their chests in gold, walked in a choreographed queue into the dining compartment.

She smiled back at them as they began arranging their burdens on the table and on the service station a few feet away. Even though domes covered the trays, the aromas struck directly to her vacant-since-she-read-Vincenzo's-email stomach, making it lament loudly.

His lips spread at the sound, his beauty supernatural in the candlelight. "Good to know you've worked up another appetite." The word *another* came out like a caress to her most intimate flesh. He was playing her body like the virtuoso he was. "Bodes well for your being more interested in food than using me for target practice."

"I see you failed to acquire harmless tableware. But you like living dangerously, don't you?" She picked up a fork, gauging its weight and center of gravity as if to estimate a perfect throw. "I mean, silver? Isn't that deadly to your kind?"

He sat back in his chair, spreading his great body, as if to let her to take aim wherever she pleased. "If I was the kind you refer to, wouldn't I be 'undying' dangerously?"

And she realized something terrible.

She was…enjoying this. This duel of words and wills. She found it exhilarating.

It shocked her because she'd never experienced anything quite like it. Certainly never with him. She'd once loved him with all her heart, lusted after him until it hurt, but she'd never really *enjoyed* being with him. Enjoyment necessitated ease, humor, and those and so much more had been missing from his life. He'd been too tense, too *in*tense, in work and in passion. She'd felt only towering yet turbulent emotions while he was around.

Now, this new him was just plain…*fun*.

Fun? The man who was more or less kidnapping her and making her marry him temporarily under terrible conditions and for all the wrong reasons while seducing her out of her mind just because he could?

Yeah. He was doing all that. And was still fun with a capital *F*. It made everything she felt for him even fiercer.

Had she caught his masochistic tendencies? Or maybe she was developing Stockholm syndrome after all?

Again unaware of her turmoil, he pursued their latest topic. "In the interest of not turning to dust if you fling something my way while you attempt to crack open the crab…" He took the fork from her, gathered the rest of her cutlery and placed them on the tray of a retreating waiter.

Admitting that there was no denying, or fighting, the enjoyment, she decided to go with the flow. As he'd recommended earlier, in what felt like another life.

She eyed him in derision. "You could have left me the spoon. It poses minimal danger, certainly a lesser one than the mess I'll make as I slurp soup directly from the bowl and wipe sauce off the plate with my fingers."

"Mess away." Another button had his chair circling the table, bringing him a breath away. "I'll lick you clean."

Leaving her struggling with another bout of arrhythmia, he leaned across her then lifted silver covers bearing Castaldini's royal insignia in repoussé, uncovering serving plates and bowls simmering over gentle flames. Her salivary glands gushed with the combination of aromas—his and the food's. He filled a bowl with heavenly smelling soup, garnishing it with dill and croutons. Then he reached across the table for his spoon.

Dipping it in the steaming depths, he scooped a spoonful then brought it to his lips. Pursing them slowly, sensuously, he blew a cooling breath over the thick creaminess. It rippled, just like the waves of arousal inside her.

Her nerves reverberated like plucked strings as he drew her to his side, no longer knowing if she felt her heart or his booming inside her rib cage. Then he lifted the spoon to her lips. They opened involuntarily, accepting his offering. She gulped down the delicious, rich liquid, moaning at the taste, at his ministrations. *Vincenzo was feeding her.*

Then he was kissing her, plumbing her depths with wrenching possession, as if he'd drink her up, gulping down her moans as they poured from her, growling the fervor of his endearments and enjoyment inside her. *"Meravigliosa, deliziosa..."*

Her stomach made another explicit protest.

He pulled back, his eyes on fire, his smile teasing. "So the flesh is willing, but the stomach is even more so. Will you stop looking so delicious so I can feed you?"

Unable to do anything but keep her head against his shoulder and her body ensconced in the security and delight of his, she sighed. "So, it's my doing now?"

"Everything is your doing, *gloriosa mia.* Everything."

For all the indulgence in which he'd said that, it confused her. For it didn't feel like a joke. Yet all she could do was surrender to his pampering and marvel at what a difference a few hours could make. She'd started this bent on resisting to the end. Now look at her. Her mind was shutting down, her will raising the white flag. And why not?

This, whatever this was, wouldn't last. But she knew that this time. She'd been forewarned, should be forearmed against any pain and disillusion. And it felt so good. The best she'd ever felt. Why not just revel in it?

Even at the cost of untold damages later? Maybe it couldn't be survived this time?

She gazed into his gorgeous eyes, let his spell topple the last pillar of her sanity, and had to face what she'd never wanted to admit. She'd missed him like she would a vital organ. The accumulated longing was only exacerbated by the new appreciation that was taking her over.

So yes. She'd take this journey with him. At any cost.

"We'll be landing in minutes, *Principe*."

The announcement made Glory do a triple take over Vincenzo's shoulder at the wall clock in the distance.

It was nine hours since they'd come on board already?

Time had never flown so imperceptibly. So pleasurably. She hadn't felt sleepy all through the flight, only deliciously languorous yet energized at once, each passing minute electrified, alive.

And here they were. Landing in a place she'd never been, and till forty-eight hours ago had thought, for too many reasons, she'd never be. His homeland. A land of vivid legend and unique tradition.

Castaldini.

She'd been so engrossed in Vincenzo and their newfound affinity she hadn't once looked outside the window as the pilot had periodically announced the landmarks they were flying over. She was now draped half over Vincenzo, one leg held in a possessive hand over his thighs, her face inches from his as they lay back on a now-reclined couch, gazing at each other, luxuriating in chatting and bickering and just relishing the hell out of each other.

Giving her thigh a gentle squeeze, he leaned in for another of those barely leashed kisses that had been scrambling her coherence, then withdrew with a regretful sigh. "Though I think some fuses inside me will burn out when I do, I have to take my hands off you. You need to see this. Castaldini from the air is breathtaking."

He untangled them and took her with him as he sat up, opening the shutter on the window behind them. He stood behind her as she rose to her knees and bent forward to peer down at his homeland. But she registered nothing but him as he pressed against her, one hand pulling her back into his hardness, the other moving the mass of her hair aside to caress her back and buttocks. All she wanted was to thrust back at him, beg him to end the torment that had been building for hours, years, plunge inside her as she knelt like that, vulnerable, open. She wished he would plummet them into delirium as they descended into his domain and the limited time they'd have together.

He bent over her until he was covering her back then suckled her earlobe, pouring his seduction right into her brain. "See this, *gloriosa mia?* This is where I'm going to make you mine again, this land that's as glorious as you are."

Everything inside her throbbed like an inflamed nerve, screaming for his invasion, his domination. "So you took your hands off me, only to substitute them with your whole body."

"Don't tell me, tell your body." His hand twisted in her hair, harnessing her as he suckled her neck, thrust against her, mimicking the act of possession. "It's operating mine remotely. It must want to keep my fuses intact, needs them fully functional." She was way past contesting this. With the way she'd been responding to his every touch, inviting more, she wondered how he hadn't taken her yet. Or why. He nipped her jaw, which sent another shock wave of need spasming in her core. "Now look."

It took moments to focus on the sight beneath her through the crimson haze of arousal. The place where she would come to life again, in his arms, in his orbit, however briefly.

And it was as he'd said. Breathtaking. Glorious.

The island gleamed like a collection of multifaceted jewels in the early afternoon sun. Jade masses of palm and olive trees, ruby and garnet rooftops on amber and moonstone houses, obsidian roads. White-gold beaches surrounded everything and were hugged in turn by the gradations of a turquoise-and-emerald Mediterranean.

Her chest tightening with elusive longing, she turned amazed eyes to him. "How can you leave this place, and stay away so long?"

Relief flared in his eyes, as if he'd been worried about her response. As if she could feel anything but wonder at beholding this magnificence.

"Wait until you see it at ground level." He turned her around, sat both of them down, buckled them in and brought her hands to his lips with a contemplative sigh. "But you're right. I was here too little for too many years."

"And now you're taking the UN post, you're going to be anywhere but here." And they wouldn't be here for their year of marriage.

As if feeling her disappointment, he shook his head. "We'll come here often and stay as long as possible each time. We can stay for a good while now. Would you like that?"

Vincenzo was asking her if she'd like to stay? When he hadn't bothered to ask if she'd like to come in the first place? Was that part of his "put her at ease" campaign?

If it was, it was succeeding. Spectacularly.

She melted back, luxuriating in his solicitude, no matter

its motives. She hadn't worked up the courage to take an active part in this seduction, but having him this close made her dizzy with the need to touch and taste him. His skin made her drool, polished as bronze, soft as satin. And it was like that everywhere. She knew. She'd once explored him inch by inch. She couldn't wait to binge on his flawlessness again.

But having taken the decision to give in to the insanity, she knew she'd have the mind-blowing pleasure soon. Sighing with the relief of surrender, she looked into his expectant eyes, loving the anxious expectation she saw there.

"As long as I can get a better toothbrush than the one in the jet's welcome pack."

Elation blazed in his eyes before he crushed her lips in an assuaging yet distressing kiss, groaning inside her. "Next time we're here, or on my jet—yes, I have only one—we're going to do our dueling and eating and bantering in bed. I hope you know what it cost me to not take you there this time."

"Because it's your king and queen's bed?"

"*Bellissima,* I'll have to refresh your memory that when it comes to taking you, I don't care where we are."

As if she needed her memory refreshed. She'd spent years wishing it erased. He'd once taken her at work, in the park, in his car, everywhere—the only uncharacteristic rule breaking he'd done back then. But…

"Then why didn't you?"

Winding a thick lock of her hair around his hand, he tugged her closer, whispered against her cheek, "Because I want to wait. For the ring. For our wedding night."

After that she had no idea what she said or what happened. Agitated all over again at being hit with the reality of what she was doing, she functioned on auto as they landed in what must have been the royal airport and disembarked.

A Mercedes was awaiting them at the bottom of the stairs.

The driver saluted Vincenzo with a deep bow, gave him the key then rushed to another car. Then Vincenzo was driving them out of the airport on a road that ran by the shore.

She gazed dazedly at the picturesque scenery as the powerful car sped on the smoothest black asphalt road she'd ever been on. She didn't ask where they were going. Now that she'd given up resisting, she wanted him to surprise her, and she had no doubt he'd keep doing that. This time she'd enjoy it. Having no expectations, knowing the worst was to come, freed her, allowing her to live in the moment.

For someone who worried every single second she was awake, and most of the moments she slept, too, it was an unknown sensation. Like free fall. And she was loving it more by the second.

Vincenzo bantered with her nonstop, acting the perfect tour guide, pointing out landmarks and telling her stories about each part of the island. He said he'd take her to Jawara, the capital, and the royal palace, later. For now, he wanted to show her something else.

Letting the magic of this land with its balmy weather and brilliant skies seep through her, she soaked up his information and consideration. Then coming around a hill, in the distance there was...

She sat up straight, her heart hammering.

This...this was his home. His ancestral home.

She'd researched this place in her greed to find out everything about him. She'd read sonnets about it, written by Moorish poets, sonnets about the princes who inhabited it, and defended and ruled the countryside at its feet. Back when she'd thought she'd meant something to him, she'd ached for the time he'd take her there, as he'd promised.

Now she knew she meant nothing to him, and he hadn't promised anything, and yet he'd just taken her there.

Life was truly incomprehensible.

Photos had conveyed a complex of buildings overlooking a tranquil sea with gorgeous surrounding nature. But its reality was way more. Layer upon layer of natural and man-made wonders stretched as far as her vision did, drenched in the Mediterranean sun and canopied by its brilliant skies.

The centerpiece of the vista was a citadel complex that crouched high on a rocky if verdant hill like something out of a fantasy. At its foothills spread a countryside so lush and a town so untouched by modernity, she felt as if they were traveling through time as they approached.

The complex sprawled on multiple levels over the rugged site, the land around it teeming with wildflowers, orange trees and elms. As they approached, Vincenzo folded back the roof so she could hear the resident mockingbirds filling the afternoon with songs. He told her they were welcoming her.

Then they were crossing an honest-to-goodness moat, and she did feel she'd crossed into a different era.

Driving through huge wooden gates, Vincenzo drove around a mosaic-and-marble fountain in a truly expansive cobblestone courtyard, parking before the central tower. He hopped out without opening his door and ran around to scoop her into his arms without opening hers.

Giggling at his boyish playfulness, she glanced around embarrassedly at the dozens of people coming and going, no doubt the caretakers of his castle, all with their gazes and grins glued on her and Vincenzo.

He climbed the ancient stone steps with her protesting that she was too heavy all the way. By the time they arrived at a stone terrace at the top, he'd proved she wasn't, for him. He was barely breathing faster. He'd always been fit. But he must have upped his exercise regimen. She couldn't wait to test his boosted stamina....

The moment he put her down on her feet, she rushed across the terrace and came up against the three-foot-high balustrade looking over the incredible vista that sprawled to the horizon. Well-being surged through her in crashing waves, making her stand on tiptoe, arch her back and open her arms wide as if to encompass the beauty around her.

Vincenzo came up behind her, stopping less than a whisper away, creating a field of screaming sensuality between them, his lips blazing a path of destruction from her temple to the swell of her breasts. By the time he took the same path back up, she was ready to beg for his touch.

She didn't have to. He finally pulled her against him, arms crisscrossing beneath breasts that felt swollen and heavy. His murmur thrummed inside her in a path that connected her heart and core, melting both. "*Dea divina mia,* my divine goddess, now I know what this place lacked in my eyes. Your beauty gracing it. I won't be able to think of this place again except as a backdrop to showcase and worship you."

That was…extravagant. When had he learned to talk like that? With the women who flowed in and out of his bed?

A fist squeezed her heart dry of beats.

Steady. She had no right to feel despondent or disillusioned. Vincenzo wasn't hers. He never had been.

But the thought still didn't sit right. Those women had always seemed as if they'd been there to serve his purpose. She couldn't see him serenading them. So where did the poetry come from? Why was he so free with it? She'd already promised him the pretense *and* the passion.

So was he only going all-out to make her feel better about both?

Yeah. That had to be it.

But he'd said his passion had always been real. Whatever his reasons for his past cruelty, it didn't matter. For now, she could have heaven.

"If you think I add to the scenery that much, I'll pose for a photo shoot if you ever need to put the place up for sale. I can see the ad with the title 'Property in Paradise.'" She turned in his arms. "But seriously, now I've seen it up close, I'm wondering how you don't live here most of the time."

"Maybe now I will." His tone remained that tempting burr. But she felt it. An earnestness. A query. One he couldn't be asking. This was a fake marriage, with a nonexistent future. He wouldn't be considering her or soliciting her endorsement before he made plans for his own future.

Ignoring a pang of regret, she pretended she didn't hear the subtext in his comment. There was probably none, anyway.

"So, what now?"

"We start preparing for next week."

"What's next week?

He pressed her against the balustrade and spanned her rib cage with his large hands, the translucence of his eyes bottomless reflections of the vivid sky. Then he said, "Our wedding."

Seven

"Our wedding?"

Vincenzo's heart dipped in his chest at the frown on Glory's face as she echoed his words.

Was she angry again? After the magical flight here, when she'd gradually relaxed, seeming to accept their situation and then enjoy being with him, he'd almost forgotten how resistant she'd been. But what if her acquiescence had been a lull, and now she'd come to her senses and would start antagonizing him again? He couldn't stomach a return to friction, would give anything for their newly forged harmony to continue. Even if it meant letting her make the decisions from now on.

She threw her hands in the air. "God, I was determined to stop repeating your words like an incredulous parrot. Then you go and say something that forces me into being one!"

She *had* sounded and looked deliciously startled frequently in the past couple of days. Was that all? She was annoyed at herself for parroting his declarations?

He watched her intently, considering his response so he wouldn't trigger a relapse into hostilities. "Why is what I just said worthy of incredulous parroting?"

"When you talk you don't hear yourself? Or was it one of the other Vincenzos who said our wedding is next week?"

Her smirk blanked out his mind with the memory of having those sassy lips beneath his, soft and pliant, burning with urgency, spilling moans of pleasure. He needed to devour them again. But he had to settle this first.

He backed her up against the balustrade, his gaze sweeping her from her piled-up hair to her turquoise stilettos, hunger an ever-expanding tide inside him. "That was the one and only Vincenzo talking. So is a week too long? I can make it sooner. I probably should. We probably wouldn't survive a week."

She picked up her dropping jaw and replaced it with a more bedeviling smirk. "It's okay, this happens with a newly installed sense of humor. Sometimes you can't turn it off. Or you're such a new user, you don't know how to. Let's hope you get the hang of it soon."

This wasn't the first time she'd made comments to that effect. Had he been that much of a humorless boor before?

He guessed so. He'd been too focused on what he'd thought paramount he'd forgotten to lighten up.

But back then he'd thought his behavior suited her, the driven, dead-serious woman he'd thought her to be. Serious about work and passion. A delightful, challenging wit hadn't been among the things he'd thought she possessed, what he'd told himself he'd have to live without, with so many qualities to make up for the deficiency. Now he realized being a sourpuss had made her turn her humor off, making him miss knowing this side of her.

How much more had he missed? Was it possible other things he'd believed about her would turn out to be as totally wrong? How, when he'd had proof of them?

No. He was leaving this alone. This bomb had already detonated once and destroyed his world around him. He wasn't lighting its fuse again.

What mattered now was that she seemed to relish his new lightheartedness. He'd never dreamed they could have anything like the time they'd spent on the flight, filled with not only mounting hunger, but escalating fun, too.

He wanted more.

He went after it.

"You're right. It's a joke thinking I can wait a few days. We'll have the wedding today."

It was exhilarating. Teasing her, soaking up her reactions, opening himself wide for her retaliations, every barb targeting his humor triggers.

She obliged him with another bull's-eye. "This is worse than anything I feared. That humor program had a virus that scrambled you up. We'll have to uninstall everything in your brain and reformat you."

He pulled her into him, groaning at the electric thrill that arced between their bodies. "I like me all scrambled up like that. So shall I rush the delivery of the catering, minister and guests? I can have everything ready by eight tonight."

She arched to look up, pressing her lushness closer to him. He'd never remained that hard, that long. And he loved it.

"So he first hits his opponents with a ludicrous offer, then, as they gasp in disbelief, he follows up with an insane one, making them grab for the ludicrous lesser evil."

"You're not an opponent."

At her raised eyebrow, though it was mocking and not cynical, he felt that nip of regret again. One that made him wish he could erase the past, both distant and recent. What he'd give to restart everything from this point, with them who they were today, with no yesterdays to muddy their enjoyment of each other, and no tomorrows to cast shadows over it.

He caressed that elegant, dense eyebrow. "Put that down before someone gets hurt. Namely me. At least more than I'm already hurting." He ground his beyond-pain hardness into her, showing her she should have mercy on him. The eyes that rivaled Castaldini's skies darkened, her body yielding, shaping itself to his seeking. Her response, as always, heightened his distress, his delight. He groaned with them both. "So you want to postpone the wedding till next week."

A choppy laugh shook those globes of perfection against his chest. How he didn't have them free of their restraints and in his hands and mouth already, he had no idea. "And *then* he makes it all sound like his opponent's decision."

"'He' has no opponents here. He's just negotiating."

"I can sniff out the faintest scent of negotiating a mile away. I can't even detect a trace now."

"It must be because I learned the undetectable negotiation method at the hands of a mistress of the art."

"Seems I didn't teach you but transferred it to you. That skill has been nowhere to be found when I most needed it."

He tugged a loose glossy lock from the satin hair that shone in his homeland's sun like burnished copper. "But 'your' decision to postpone is well-advised. Next week's forecast says it will be a perfect day for a wedding."

She curled that dewy, edible lip. "Every day is a perfect day on Castaldini. But…" Something like panic spurted in her eyes. "You're serious, aren't you?" At his nod, she grabbed his lapels. "And what do you mean *wedding?*"

It was his eyebrows' turn to shoot up. "The word has more meanings than the one agreed on since the dawn of humanity?"

She shook her head, something frantic creeping into her eyes. "I thought we were just going to get a ring, sign a marriage certificate and report to the king so he can officially send you to your UN post."

It pained him that she expected only a cold ritual to befit the barren deal he'd proposed forty-eight hours ago.

Sorrow filled him for what should have been with this woman his heart and body had chosen, but wasn't and wouldn't be.

Suddenly, all levity drained from him, loosening his embrace.

Unable to remain in such intimate contact with her anymore, he stepped away. And saw it. A quiver of insecurity. A crack in the veneer of confidence and cheek.

He should have felt that was the least she deserved. To suffer some uncertainty and trepidation. But he didn't. It hurt him to see her looking so…bereft. He hated to see vulnerability in those indomitable eyes.

He forced himself to smile at her, to reach a soothing hand to her cheek. "If you didn't think I was talking about a wedding with all the trimmings, why were you surprised at all when I said next week? Or today? The ceremony you describe could have been concluded in a couple of hours."

"Forgive me if I'm boggled by the idea of *any* brand of ceremony. I was never married before, you know, for real or for pretense, and a date, let alone one so soon, makes me feel this is actually happening."

He watched her lips shaking, attempting a smile of bravado and failing, and could no longer deny it.

His gut was having a fit, sanctioning no evidence but what it sensed. It insisted she wasn't the hardened manipulator he'd once thought her. That person would have grabbed his deal, would now be working his evident eagerness to milk more from him. But she wasn't. She was really shaken.

And for the first time, he put himself in her place. Taken away from everything she knew to a strange land, her choice stripped away, her family not only unable to come to her aid, but the reason for her predicament. Her only company and precarious support was the man behind it all. And he kept blowing hot and cold, to boot. She must be feeling lost, helpless. And to a woman who'd been mistress of her own fate for so long, that must be the scariest thing she'd ever experienced.

His gut finally communicated with his brain, reaching a decision.

If he took out the terrible blot of her betrayal from their lives, he could connect the woman he'd once loved with this woman he laughed so easily with, the woman he now wanted more than he'd known he was capable of wanting. And he didn't want that woman to be under any form of compulsion.

Taking another step back, severing any intimacy, he exhaled. "It doesn't have to happen."

More uncertainty flooded her eyes. "What do you mean?"

"I mean you don't have to marry me."

Glory wondered if the sun had overheated her brain.

That would explain feeling and hearing things that couldn't be real. When Vincenzo had stepped away, she'd felt as if she was teetering on a cliff without his support. Then, because of the distance that had come over him, she'd felt she'd fallen into the abyss of the past, discarded all over again.

That remoteness couldn't have been real. Not after all his pursuit and passion. And he couldn't have just said…

"I don't have to marry you?" There she went, parroting him again. She swallowed the knot of anxiety that rose in her throat. "Just a minute ago you wanted me to marry you in seven hours or seven days, and now… Just what are you playing at?"

He stuffed his hands into his pockets. "Nothing. No more games, Glory. But don't worry. I'll still help your family. Of course, they can never again as much as forge a note to your nephew's kindergarten or take a cent from a tip dish."

Her heart slowed, as if fearing every beat would make

this real. "Y-you mean that?" His slow nod, his solemn gaze
cleaved into her. "Wh-what will you do about King Ferruccio's decree?"

"I don't know. I'm thinking on the fly here. Maybe I'll
ask someone else."

Her heart boomed now, each beat almost tearing it apart.
She couldn't bear thinking he'd marry someone else, even
in pretense. "Why?"

His shrug was heavy; his spectacular face gripped in the
brooding she hadn't seen there since she'd met him again. "It
just suddenly hit me, how wrong this whole thing is."

It suddenly hit her, too. That he wasn't only confounding.
He was nerve-racking. Heartbreaking. And he probably did
suffer from a severe bipolar disorder. What else explained
the violent pendulum of his mood swings?

He forced out an exhalation. "You can go back as soon
as you wish. If you want me to escort you, I will. If not, the
royal jet is at your disposal."

Feeling as if her whole world was being swept from under
her, she leaned back on the balustrade before she collapsed.

He meant it. He was setting her free.

But she didn't want to be free.

She no longer knew what to do with her freedom.

Before he'd reinvaded her life, she'd spent years nurtur-
ing the illusion of steadiness. His hurricane had uprooted
her simulated peace and exposed the truth of her chaos, the
bleakness of her isolation.

But she'd already succumbed and had woven a tapestry of
expectations around this time she would have had with him.
She'd anticipated its rejuvenation, thought it would see her
through the rest of her life. In her worst estimations she'd
never thought it would all end before it began.

But it had. He'd suddenly cut her loose, letting her plummet back into her endless spiral of nothingness.

She pushed away from the balustrade as if from a precipice and past the monolith who stood brooding down at her.

She looked around her stunning surroundings, every nerve burning with despondency.

In a different life, Vincenzo would have brought her here because he wanted to share his home with her. If not permanently, then at least sincerely, passionately, for as long the fates let them be together.

In this life, he'd brought her here for all the wrong reasons, only to send her away before she got more than a tantalizing taste of the place that had forged him into the man she loved.

Yes, in spite of the insanity and self-destructiveness of it all, she still loved him.

Now she'd only gotten enough of a glimpse of him in his element to live with their memory gnawing at her, to mourn what hadn't and could never have been.

Needing to get it over with, she turned and found him still standing where he had been, his back to her, looking up at the sky. Thunder filled her ears as her gaze ached over the sight of his majestic figure…then she realized.

The din didn't come from her stampeding heart. It was coming from above.

It took a moment to realize its direction then see its origin. A helicopter.

"The Castaldinian Air Force One, rotorcraft edition." Vincenzo gazed at her over his shoulder, his eyes grave. "Seems Ferruccio couldn't wait to meet my future bride."

Hot needles sprouted behind her eyes. She didn't want to meet anyone. She wasn't even a counterfeit bride now.

He turned, expression wiped clean. "Please say nothing while he's here. I'll resolve things with him later."

She only nodded numbly, making no reaction when he took her hand and led her from the terrace and down the stairs he'd carried her up what felt like a lifetime ago.

By the time they exited the castle, the helicopter was landing in the courtyard, the revolving blades spraying the fountain water at them. Glory shuddered at the touch of the warm mist, cold spreading in her bones.

As the rotors slowed down, a man stepped down from the pilot's side. She recognized him on sight. So the king flew himself here. And without guards or fanfare. It said so much about him and his status in Castaldini.

But all photos and footage hadn't done him justice. He'd looked exceptional in those. But the man was way more than that. He was on par with Vincenzo in looks and physique. He could even pass for his brother.

King Ferruccio rushed in strides laden with urgency and power to the passenger side as it opened. In moments, his arms went around the waist of a golden vision of a woman, lifting her down as if he was handling his own heart.

"And the king has brought his queen," she heard Vincenzo mutter over the rotor's dying whirs. "Or maybe it's the other way around. She must be thrilled to see me entering the gilded cage at last."

Glory's heart contracted on what felt like thorns on hearing his words, and more as she watched the regal couple advance hand in hand, their bond blatant in their every nuance.

What attention they didn't have focused on each other, they had trained on her. She looked from one to the other, feeling like a specimen under a microscope.

Queen Clarissa was what Glory had always imagined fairy queens to look like. In a sleeveless floor-length lilac dress and high-heeled matching sandals, she stood maybe an inch or two taller than Glory, with the body of a woman who'd been ripened by the satisfaction and pampering of a powerful man's constant passion, by bearing his children. From the top of her golden head to her toes, she glowed in the afternoon sun as if she was made of its radiance. Glory could easily believe she had angels in her lineage.

King Ferruccio was as tall as Vincenzo, another overpoweringly handsome D'Agostino. There was no doubt the same blood ran in their veins. They had almost identical coloring, too. But that was where the similarities ended.

While Vincenzo was imposing, Ferruccio was intimidating. If his wife was the benevolent breed of angel, he was the avenging variety. And it had nothing to do with the way he looked. It was in his eyes. His vibe. This was a man who'd seen and done unspeakable things…and had those things done to him. Which made sense. He'd grown up an illegitimate boy on the streets, one who'd dragged himself from the dirt to the very top. She could only imagine what he'd been through, what had shaped him into the man who was now undisputedly the best king in Castaldini's history. She felt no one could know the scope of his depths, and those of his sufferings and complexities.

No one but his wife, that was.

They seemed to share a soul.

It hurt to see them together, to feel the love arcing between them in a closed circuit of harmony. What she'd once thought she'd had with Vincenzo.

Vincenzo, who was still holding her hand as they stopped two feet away from the couple, making her feel as if he couldn't let go of it. When he was letting her go completely.

Hand still entwined with hers Vincenzo bowed before his king and queen, his other hand flat palmed over his heart, in the Castaldinian royal salute.

What was she supposed to do? Bow, too? Curtsy?

Before her muscles unlocked, Vincenzo straightened, his face softening on a smile that she'd only seen before when he'd been talking about Clarissa.

With an arm going around her waist, he gave Queen Clarissa a tender hug with his other arm, kissing her gently on her cheek, before raising one eyebrow at King Ferruccio. "I see you've brought your husband with you."

So he was on teasing terms with his king. Figured. It was clear that though he observed the king's status officially, he was on the same level personally.

Clarissa chuckled, her thick, long hair blowing around her face in the breeze like strands of sunlight. "You know me, I can't say no to him."

Vincenzo's lips twisted. "I can train you."

Her chuckle turned to a snicker. "Like *you* can say no to him."

Vincenzo teased. "I'm not the woman who has the power to make a yo-yo out of His Majesty. It's your duty as his queen to save his subjects from his implacability, and as his wife to counteract the toxic level of yeses in his blood."

Clarissa gave her husband a look full of all they had between them. "I like him intoxicated." She turned teasing eyes on Vincenzo. "Now shush, Cenzo, and let me meet your much better half."

Then she turned those eyes on Glory. They were so unbelievable, Glory involuntarily stepped closer to find out if they were contacts. They weren't. She'd seen so-called violet eyes before, always blue with a violet tinge. But Clarissa's were pure, luminescent amethysts. Eyes to stare into for hours. Ferruccio evidently wanted to do nothing else for life.

Glory's lips trembled on a smile in response to Clarissa's exquisite one as she clasped her in a warm, fragrant embrace.

Already on the brink of tears, Clarissa's words almost made them escape. "Welcome to Castaldini and to the family, Glory. I'm thrilled to have another friend my age, especially since I hear we have so much in common, our professional training—" she pulled back, her smile becoming mischie-

vous "—and being married to one of our impossible yet ir-
resistible D'Agostino men."

In spite of her upheaval, her lips moved of their own accord. "Your Majesty…"

Clarissa held out a warning finger. "Stop right there! No
YMs and not the *Q* word, either. Away from all the court
stuff, I'm just Rissa—my husband claims exclusivity on Clarissa—" another melting look at her husband "—and I'm just
part of a brigade around here, with the other members being
Gabrielle, my brother Durante's wife; Phoebe, my cousin Leandro's; and Jade, my cousin Eduardo's. We used to call our-
selves the Fabulous Four. Now we'll be the Fabulous Five."

Glory swallowed, at a loss on how to answer. Seemed Vincenzo's advice about saying nothing was the best one to follow in this mess. She smiled weakly at Clarissa, wishing the
earth actually opened and swallowed people.

"You're real."

The deep, dark burr had goose bumps storming across her
body. King Ferruccio.

Without coming closer, he made her feel his presence had
enveloped her, immobilizing her for analysis as he cocked
his head in contemplation. "I thought Vincenzo was pulling
one over on me until I was forced to send him off to his new
post, only to discover too late that you were a figment of his
very creative mind."

Her bones tightened under his scrutiny. He felt something
wasn't right. His eyes said he *knew* it. Shrewd man. That must
be how he'd raised himself from destitute illegitimacy to become not only one of the world's most hard-hitting magnates,
but the king who'd brought Castaldini back from the brink of
ruin and into unprecedented prosperity in under four years.
The intelligence she felt radiating from him was almost fright-
ening, and he must possess all the additional qualities that
made others follow him.

Under his probing, words formed on her lips. "I am real, I assure you, Your Majesty. Forgive me if I won't call you Ruccio, if that's your name in informal setting, according to the abbreviations I observed your names undergo."

A ghost of a smile played on Ferruccio's uncompromising lips. "Come to think of it, that contraction should have been my name's fate. Seems no one was bold enough to attempt it. But you can call me Ferruccio like everyone is free to, since my wife has her own exclusive names for me. But Your Majesty is certainly not something you're allowed to use."

Her smile attempted a semblance of steadiness. "It might be impossible to call you by your name just like that."

Ferruccio's gaze leveled on her. "In her incurable kindness, Clarissa has made it a request, but I have no such qualms. Away from the court I order you to call me Ferruccio. As your future king, that's a royal decree."

"See what I have to put up with?"

That was Vincenzo, his tone light and teasing, but his eyes made her feel he was following her breaths.

Ignoring him, Ferruccio maintained his focus on her. "But you're not only real, you're nothing like I expected. As soon as I had a name to his alleged fiancée, I investigated you." At Clarissa's silent reprimand, he caressed the hand that discreetly poked at him, his eyes on Glory. "And now I'm left with an unsolvable question. How was he able to get a woman of your caliber not only to take him seriously, but to agree, and so fast, to take on the onerous task of marrying him?"

Vincenzo snorted a laugh. "And that's what you say when you're trying your best to marry me off? What would you have said if you wanted to send her running away screaming?"

Clarissa tugged on her husband arm, her color high with embarrassment. "He must have done exactly what you did to make me undertake the same task with you." Her eyes turned apologetically on Glory. "Now you see the *impossible* part I was talking about."

Suddenly deciding to throw herself into the part Vincenzo expected her to play until his king and queen left, Glory quirked her lips at Clarissa. "And now that I do, I actually feel better about Vincenzo's exasperating tendencies. I now have proof they're genetic and therefore beyond his control."

Clarissa whooped with laughter. "I *knew* it! I liked you on sight, but now I know I'll *love* you! You're exactly the addition we need to our brigade!"

Ferruccio cast an indulgent look at his wife, then raised an eyebrow at Glory, clearly approving the comeback that bundled him and Vincenzo and put them firmly in their places.

Vincenzo's arm tightened. "How about we call it quits, Ferruccio, before we're cut down to an even tinier size?"

Ferruccio gave a tiny bow of his regal head. "By all means. Not that I'll quit being flabbergasted at your phenomenal luck anytime soon."

Vincenzo sighed. "Your flattery knows no bounds. Now before you have Glory rethinking her hasty and ill-advised decision to marry me, how about you go do some kingly stuff and leave me to resume what I was about to do before your... surprise inspection? I was about to take Glory to explore the place before dinner." He turned his eyes to Clarissa. "You, of course, are more than welcome to join us."

Clarissa looked up into her husband's eyes, exchanging what Glory had once thought she'd shared with Vincenzo. Such allegiance. Such understanding. Such adoration.

Clarissa pinched her husband's hard cheek. "See what you've done? Now make nice so you can stay for the tour and dinner, too."

Catching her hand to bury his lips in its palm, Ferruccio looked over at Vincenzo challengingly. "Why make nice when I can order him to invite me? Or better still, invite myself?"

Vincenzo raised him a pitying glance. "Seems you haven't lived on Castaldini long enough to realize how provincial it remains, don't realize what power I wield in my ancestral region. Here, I rule supreme. King or no, Ferruccio, one more word and I sic my whole province on you."

Ferruccio's eyes gleamed with devilry. "Let's not start a civil war over the dinner you've been cornered into feeding me. Now lead the way, Vincenzo. And try to do your 'ancestral home' justice as you act as the guide."

Grumbling something about getting Ferruccio later when he wasn't under Clarissa's protection, Vincenzo did lead the way.

And how he did. He detailed everything with the thoroughness of someone who took the utmost pride in the place that had been in his family for generations. As he should. This place was phenomenal.

And it would be the first and last time she was here. Why not just enjoy the experience while it lasted?

"The architecture of all the buildings is a symbiosis of every culture that makes up Castaldini—Roman, Andalusian, Moorish and some North African influences," Vincenzo said, his explanations all for her. "Geometric patterns rule, with accessory-heavy decoration, from mosaic to plaster carving to worked metal. The main castle is circular but the other annexed buildings and towers are quadrangular, with all rooms opening onto inner courts."

It was all right out of a fairy tale. Far grander and better preserved that any of the architectural wonders she'd visited all over the world.

She asked, "How long has this place been in your family?"

"Over five hundred years."

Wow. That really put into perspective the difference between them. Her family tree was known only three or four generations back on both sides. And there hadn't been a "family home" in her life, let alone an ancestral one.

Vincenzo underlined the unbridgeable gap between them. "My umpteenth great-grandfather was Castaldini's founder, King Antonio D'Agostino."

"*Our* umpteenth great-grandfather," Ferruccio put in.

Vincenzo countered, "*My* line is that of one of his grandsons, who started building this place, but it reached its present size by gradual additions of more quadrangles over two centuries. Leandro, a slightly less obnoxious cousin, inherited a similar place, which King Antonio himself had built. When we were young, we always liked to brag about which is bigger and better."

Glory's blood tumbled as her imagination flew on a tangent, to other bigger and better…things.

"You still do," Ferruccio said, his tone condescending. "I always leave you boys to squabble over size and quality. Mine is the undisputed best of all."

"But the royal palace isn't yours, my liege," Vincenzo calmly retorted. "As per Castaldini's laws, you're just the resident caretaker. You really should start building or acquiring a place to pass on to your children."

Ferruccio suddenly threw his head back and guffawed. "See that, Vincenzo? That's the take-no-prisoners attitude I want you to have when you're representing Castaldini."

Clarissa's eyes rounded. "You mean you've been poking him to get him to bare his fangs?"

Ferruccio grinned down at her. "He's been getting soft of late. Now that he has Glory, I was afraid he'd turn to putty and be no good to me in the war zone I'm sending him to. I had to do something to remind him how to use his fangs."

Vincenzo huffed. "Have I told you lately how much I love you, Ferruccio?"

"You're welcome to renew your oath of allegiance any-time, Vincenzo."

Clarissa spluttered as she smacked her husband and cousin playfully, and Glory had to join in the laughter.

After that the day flowed, filled with many unprecedented experiences with the most exciting people she'd ever met.

It was past midnight when she and Vincenzo stood in the courtyard, watching the regal couple vanish into the night.

Her heart twisted at the symbolism. This place and Vincenzo would soon disappear from her life as if they'd never been.

The moment she turned to Vincenzo, he turned to her, too, taking a leashed step closer, practically vibrating with intensity.

And she realized. That he was sending her away because he no longer wanted to coerce her. But he still wanted her. And she'd already decided that this passion was worth any risk.

Closing the gap between them, taking both his hands in hers, she took the plunge into the path to eventual heartache.

And she whispered, "I'll marry you for the year you need, Vincenzo. My choice this time."

Eight

"What did you say?"

As the exclamation rang in her ear, Glory sighed. "You heard right, Mom. I'm getting married. To Vincenzo."

Silence expanded on the other end of the line.

Which was to be expected. She herself still couldn't believe any of this was really happening.

After she'd told Vincenzo last night that she'd marry him of her own free will, she hadn't known what to expect.

Or she had. She'd expected him to be elated, or relieved, or best scenario of all, to resume his mind-melting seduction.

He'd done none of that. He'd just taken her hands to his lips, murmured a cell-scrambling *"Grazie mille, gloriosa mia"* then he'd silently led her to her guest quarters and bid her good-night.

After a night of tossing and turning and pacing her quarters, which looked like something out of a fairy tale, he'd come knocking with a breakfast tray. He didn't stay, said he had too many things to prepare. He asked her to invite everyone she wanted and to make lists of what she needed for the wedding. It *would* be in a week's time.

The first person she'd thought of had been her mother.

And here she was, pretending this was real to the person she was closest to in the world. But there was nothing to be gained by telling her mother the truth. Her mother had suffered too much, and God only knew how long her remission would last this time—or if it would. She would do and say anything to make her mother as happy as possible for as long as she could.

Glenda Monaghan's silence thickened until it weighed down on her. "Mom, you still there?"

A ragged exhalation. "Yes, darling. I'm just…surprised."

Her mother had been apprehensive about her first liaison with Vincenzo. She had feared Glory would end up plummeting into the huge gap in power and status between them. But on meeting Vincenzo, Glenda had thought him magnificent and later waxed poetic about the purity and clarity of his emotions for Glory. She suspected her mother had entertained dreams that her daughter would become a princess and had looked devastated when Glory had informed her that the relationship was over.

Glenda must be stunned her dream was coming true after all these years, and so suddenly. When they'd talked four days ago, none of this had been on the horizon.

Glory gave her mother a pretty little story about how she and Vincenzo had met again, rediscovering how they'd once felt about each other and resolving the issues that had separated them. This time, he'd popped the question and wanted to get married right away so he could start his new post with them as husband and wife.

By the time she'd told all those lies, Glory was almost panting, but she forced herself to go on. "Vincenzo will send his private jet for you. If you can come right away, I'd love it! If not, come a couple of days before the wedding if possible, to help me with all the last-minute things. All you need to do is buy something pretty to wear and pack a bag for two weeks or so. You should enjoy Castaldini at least that long."

When she finished, silence stretched again.

Then her mother whispered, "Is it only me you're inviting?"

Glory had known that question would come yet still wasn't ready to answer it.

From the time Glory was a little girl, her mother had tried all she could to defuse her dissatisfaction with her father and brother. Then, in the past few years, she'd fought to reinstate the relationship that Glory had escaped, always ready with an excuse for their latest damaging decisions or exasperating actions. Now the situation was reversed and it was Glory who had to hide the true extent of her father's and brother's transgressions from her mother. And she wasn't sure she could do that if she saw them again now.

But her established disapproval wasn't grave enough to warrant not inviting them to her wedding. If she didn't invite them, she'd have to give her mother an explanation why. She couldn't tell the truth. And she'd already told her enough lies.

But then, why not just have them here? She doubted she'd have enough mental or emotional energy to register their presence. And Vincenzo had stressed she could invite anyone. By "anyone" she believed he sanctioned her father's and brother's presence. And she did want to please her mom.

She forced lightness in her voice. "You're the one I can't wait to have here, but of course Dad and Daniel are invited." That didn't sound as welcoming as she'd tried to make it. Well, her father and brother would just have to make do with that level of enthusiasm.

"Don't you want your father to give you away, darling? I

know it's been a long while since you thought he was the best dad in the world, but he does try."

Yeah, he tried so hard his efforts could send him to prison for life. "I'm almost thirty, Mom. I'm perfectly capable of walking down that aisle on my own."

"I know you can do anything on your own, darling, but your father has dreamed of this day for so long, and—" her mother broke off, as if swallowing tears "—it'll break his heart."

Glory gritted her teeth on the surge of familiar guilt she suffered every time she felt she'd been too hard on her father. But once the sentimental reaction subsided she always realized that she hadn't been. If only she'd been harder, had known the truth earlier, she could have stopped him and Daniel from spiraling that far that they risked their freedom. There was one way out of this for now.

"Listen, Mom, I'm marrying a prince from a kingdom steeped in history and tradition and giving me away might not be part of the ritual here. If it is, I'll let Dad give me away."

Another fraught silence greeted her prevaricating promise. For an otherwise shrewd woman, her mother had a rationalizing disease where her husband and son were concerned. Glory barely suppressed her need to tell her mother to open her eyes and see her husband and son for the lost causes they were.

The one thing that had always held her back was knowing how much they loved her mother. Glory had no doubt they'd die for her mother in a heartbeat.

What an inextricable mess everyone was tangled up in.

Sighing, she soothed her mother. "Just pack your men up and bring them here, Mom. It'll all work out."

After that, she diverted her mom into talking about the guest list and wedding plans.

By the time Glory ended the call, she felt she'd run a mile. Now on to the marathon of the next week.

* * *

After sunset, just as she was getting restless having nothing to do, Vincenzo came into her suite. He introduced the tall, graceful and extremely chic man with him as his valet and right-hand man, Alonzo Barbieri. After greeting her in utmost delight and kissing her hand as if she was his long-lost princess, Alonzo ushered in four other people, two men and two women, each carrying a heavy, ornate antique chest. They opened them on the coffee table then promptly left, leaving her gaping at the contents.

The freaking royal jewels of Castaldini.

She'd thought they would be— No, she couldn't have thought anything that could come close to—to...*that.*

Each piece on its own would have been jaw-dropping, but having them piled together—from hefty necklaces, bracelets and tiaras to intricate earrings, brooches and rings—the treasure was literally dazzling. There were even some scepters and goblets and ornamental pieces not for wearing. And were those...those...

"The royal crowns! What are those doing here?"

As she turned stunned eyes between the two men, it was Alonzo who supplied an explanation. "I applaud your knowledge of our history, *Principessa!*" Before she could wince at the title, he went on, "Those are indeed the crowns that had been worn by kings and queens of Castaldini until King Benedetto and his wife—Queen Clarissa's father and mother. But since their lives were marked by tragedy, King Ferruccio had new crowns made, with personalized changes, so the past wouldn't throw the least shadow on his and Queen Clarissa's lives."

More proof of how total Ferruccio's love for Clarissa was.

With that strange reticence that had come over him still subduing his eyes, Vincenzo said, "As my princess you're entitled to any piece you'd like. After last night, Ferruccio and Clarissa insist you should have as *many* as you'd like."

Alonzo chuckled. "They're ready to offer the whole treasure to you as the one who'll save *Principe* Vincenzo from unremitting bachelorhood. I am also offering whatever your heart desires for that Herculean achievement."

So Vincenzo hadn't even taken his closest person into his confidence. Alonzo clearly believed this was a grand love story with a happily ever after.

"Ferruccio is also putting the royal palace and everyone inside it at your service," Vincenzo said.

"He wants us to have the wedding there?"

Vincenzo nodded. "Being the control freak that he is, he insists I take my vows under his supervision."

"Can't we…" She stopped, swallowed. "Can't we have the wedding here?"

A flare of surprise then intentness incinerated the deadness in Vincenzo's eyes. "Is this what you want?"

Feeling suddenly shy and awkward, wanting to smack herself for behaving as if she was a real bride, she murmured, "It's just this place is magnificent, and it's your family home…"

Vincenzo spoke over her, his tone urgent. "If it's what you want, then we certainly will have the wedding here."

Alonzo looked scandalized. "But what about King Ferruccio's decree? And all this talk about being a knight in his round table and doing anything he commands?"

Vincenzo had said that about Ferruccio? Watching those two together, you'd never have guessed he felt that way about him.

Vincenzo twisted his lips at Alonzo. "That's until my bride says different. Then it's her desires that I follow, nobody else's, no matter who they are."

Alonzo whooped. "*That's* what I waited two decades to

hear. *Principessa,* you're a miracle worker. A miracle, period."

Feeling tears too near the surface, she wanted to get this over with. "Will you please do the honors, Vincenzo? I'm almost afraid to look at those pieces, I'm not about to go rummaging through them and chip or crack something."

Vincenzo's expression hovered on the smile she'd been missing, had even gotten dependent on basking in it. "Rummage away. Those pieces have weathered the test of hundreds of years. Choose whatever you want."

"I want you—" her voice trembled, holding back *only you* "—to choose the ring for me."

A moment of probing stillness. "Are you sure?" A tinge of teasing said *after all the fuss?* Then his lips spread. "I do have one ring, one collection in mind. I always felt it was made as a tribute to the beauty of your eyes."

He gave Alonzo a nod, and as if Alonzo knew exactly which pieces Vincenzo was talking about, Alonzo started sorting through the treasure. In minutes, without letting her see what he'd selected, Alonzo placed the pieces in a rectangular box he'd had under his armpit all along then handed it to Vincenzo.

Coming to stand above where she sat feeling as though she'd fall apart any moment, Vincenzo suddenly dropped down on one knee in front of her.

Holding her stunned gaze with eyes roiling like thunderclouds, he opened the navy blue velvet box. She relinquished his gaze to its contents…and the gasp that had caught in her chest when he'd knelt before her escaped.

A seven-piece set—necklace, bracelet, ring, earrings, tiara, armlet and anklet—lay on the dark velvet like a brilliant constellation of stars set against a night sky. They were all made from the most delicate filigree yellow gold she'd ever seen, and studded with magnificent white and blue diamonds in ingenious patterns. But it was the ring that her eyes couldn't leave. A flawless, vivid blue diamond of at least ten carats, the color of her eyes at night, with emerald-cut white diamonds on both the sides.

Vincenzo singled it out, turned his hand up, asking for hers. She placed it there without volition or hesitation.

The moment he slipped the ring on her finger, she knew what a huge mistake she was committing. She wouldn't survive losing him this time.

His watchfulness intensified as he singed her hand in a kiss, then with a long groan, he stabbed his other hand into the depths of her hair and hauled her against him, kissing her so deeply, so hungrily, she felt he might finish her.

Surrendering to his passion, her need, her panic subsided as she accepted that if she wasn't careful, he *would* finish her.

"We have only one hour left to go."

Glory turned her head at Alonzo's declaration. The man was the most outstanding organizer she'd ever seen. He'd marshaled everyone's efforts to get the most efficient operation going. And in just one week, he'd managed to plan a wedding more incredible than any in storybooks.

Alonzo took exception to her saying that. The wedding hadn't happened yet, and would she stop jinxing it?

If only he knew a jinx wasn't needed to spoil anything. Everything would self-destruct in a year.

But a year was a long time.

The week had passed faster than she could catch her breath. Now the wedding was an hour away.

Her mother had arrived only yesterday with her father and brother, and Alonzo had promptly swept them off their feet and into the rush of preparations, for which Glory was grateful. No one had time to think of any relationship issues. Amelia, who'd arrived the day after Glory had invited her, had been running interference for her whenever any awkward moment arose.

Clarissa and Gabrielle—Clarissa's sister-in-law—were now flitting about doing Alonzo's last-minute bidding. He'd already sent Phoebe and Jade, the other two in the Fabulous Five brigade, on errands. Though they were his queen and princesses, in those wedding preparations, he ruled supreme.

Everything around the castle and the town below now echoed the themes of Glory's dress and accessories. Everything was swathed in glorious white, gold and a whole range of vivid blues. Vincenzo had already told her that *she* was made of Castaldini's hues, her hair of its soil, her skin of its sunlight, and her eyes of its skies.

"You do look like a princess, darling."

Glory looked at her mother in the Andalusian-style full-length mirror before shifting her gaze to stare at her reflection. She had to admit her mother was right.

So clothes did make the woman. This dress made her feel like a different person. The person a dozen designers had turned her into as she'd stood for endless hours for them to mold this creation on her.

During the stages of its creation, she hadn't imagined how it would look finished. She'd last seen it when it had yet to be embroidered. The end product was astounding.

In sweeping gradations of brilliant blues on a base of crisp white, it looked like something made in another realm, from materials and colors that defied the laws of nature. Its fitted, off-the-shoulder bodice with a heart-shaped plunging neckline accentuated her curves and swells to beyond perfection, nipping her waist to a size she hadn't believed achievable—and without a breath-stealing corset.

Her one request had been that the dress not have a mushrooming skirt. But it was only when Clarissa had backed up her request that the designers had backed down. On hearing that they hadn't taken her request as a command, Vincenzo had fired them and gotten new ones who'd been doing everything she said before she finished saying it.

Now the dress had a skirt that molded to her hips before flaring gently in layers of chiffon, tulle and lace overlaying a base of silk. The whole dress was adorned in thousands of sequins and diamonds that echoed the colors of her jewelry, in patterns that swept around her body and down the dress and formed the crest of Vincenzo's province, where he was the lord.

Alonzo finished adjusting the layered veil from the back of her high chignon, then the tiara just behind her coiffed bangs, while Amelia hooked her twenty-foot train.

As they all pulled back to exclaim over her perfection, her mother neared, tears running down her thin cheeks. "Oh, darling, I can't tell you how happy…how happy…"

A surge of poignancy threatened to fill Glory's eyes, too, as her mother choked. She blinked it back. The last thing she wanted was to go to Vincenzo with swollen eyes and reddened nose. But there was something in her mother's eyes that gripped her heart in anxiety. Something dark and regretful.

Gathering herself, her mother continued, "I'm so happy I lived to see this day, to see you with the man who loves you and who will protect you for the rest of your life."

Alarm detonated in Glory's chest. Had her mother had a relapse and not told her? She'd always said the worst thing about having cancer was how it pained Glory and disrupted her life as she'd dropped everything and rushed to her side.

Before she could blurt out her worries, a burst of music shook the chamber.

"Ferruccio has brought out the whole royal brass orchestra to your door, Glory." Clarissa chuckled at her astonishment. "It's a royal tradition in all huge occasions, playing the anthem to herald the beginning of ceremonies. And Vincenzo getting married is certainly huge."

Another wave of anxiety drenched her. This was really happening. She had to walk out now and marry Vincenzo in a legendary ceremony in front of thousands of people.

She turned away from everyone, inhaling a steadying breath as she faced herself in the mirror one last time. She wondered if everyone saw what she saw. A woman lost in love but resigned that love would remain lost to her forever?

No, they didn't. Everyone behaved as if they had no doubt this was a match made in heaven, and made forever.

Alonzo touched her shoulder gently. "Are you ready for your groom?"

She wasn't ready. For anything. Yet she was ready for nothing else, ready for everything. She nodded.

Alonzo rushed to the table where he'd arranged the blown-glass bottles filled with the aromatic oils he'd rubbed on her pulse points as Castaldinian custom dictated. He picked up one of the oils and also took the crystal pitcher filled with the rose water he'd given her earlier to drink as another part of the ritual before rushing to open the door.

Her heart clanged, expecting to see Vincenzo. The father giving the bride away wasn't done in Vincenzo's province, thankfully. Instead, the groom came to take his bride from among her family and friends, to claim her as his, and take her from her old life to the new one with him.

Everything inside her stilled as she stared at the empty doorway. Vincenzo wasn't there, and Alonzo was pouring water in his hand and sprinkling it across her doorstep carefully, once, twice, three times.

"That's to ward away evil spirits that might try to enter with your groom and conspire to come between you later," Gabrielle explained, a red-haired beauty whom the matron-of-honor dress suited best, with her eyes reflecting its sapphire and cerulean colors. She grinned sheepishly at Glory's wide-eyed stare. "I've been investigating the myriad provincial traditions around here. I'm thinking of writing a book."

"You should," Clarissa exclaimed. "You'd be even more of a national treasure if you do!"

Amelia, who was having the time of her life rubbing shoulders with a posse of princesses, chuckled. "Make it a royal decree that she must, Clarissa. With all the fascinating stuff Alonzo introduced us to during the preparations, I can't wait to read that book. I want to adopt all of those traditions in my own wedding!"

Glory barely heard their banter, all her senses focused on the threshold as Alonzo stood to one side, pumping his chest in deference and pride and called out, *"Avanti, Principe."*

And Vincenzo appeared.

His gaze slammed into hers, compacting the dozens of feet between them, making her feel him against her, his breath hovering a gasp away from her inflamed flesh.

Air vanished from the world. Fire flooded her limbs.

And that was before she really looked at him.

Her heart emptied its beats in a mad rush.

This was Vincenzo as he was born to be. As she'd never seen him before. The prince whose blood ran thick with nobility and entitlement. The man who inhabited a realm she should have never seen, let alone entered. But she had entered it once, tangentially. Now she was stumbling all the way in, even if for only a year.

Her ravenous gaze devoured his every detail. His lavish costume complemented her dress, magnifying his height, breadth and bulk, worshipping his coloring and lines. A mid-thigh jacket in royal-blue silk, embroidered with Castaldinian designs, opened over a crisp white satin shirt and golden sash. His black fitted pants disappeared into knee-high shining black leather boots. A gold cape embroidered in blues and white flowed at his back down to his calf and completed the image of an otherworldly prince.

She'd always thought no description did him justice. Seemed there were always new heights to the injustice. Of his beauty. Of his escalating effect on her.

And he was hers. Tonight. And for a whole year.

Alonzo gave him the same water he'd given her to drink, and Gabrielle whispered that now the evil spirits couldn't come between them from the inside.

Vincenzo strode in, a predator who had his prey standing before him. His eyes swept her before returning to her face with a promise that turned her into a mass of tremors.

And that was before he stopped before her and said, "I'll kick these helpful ladies out and take the edge off so I can survive the torturous festivities ahead."

The wild gleam in his eyes told her he wasn't joking. He wanted to take her now, hard and fast.

Her lungs emptied on a ragged gasp. "Vincenzo…"

"Don't stand there devouring your bride with looks and intentions." That was Clarissa, her voice merry. She must have guessed what Vincenzo was saying. "The sooner you're done with the ceremony, the sooner you can devour her for real."

Unable to blush any deeper, she watched Vincenzo turn to his queen with a glare, felt him vibrating with control as he offered her his arm.

She clung to it as if to a raft in a stormy sea, felt his power moving her legs and his support holding her up as they exited the chamber after another water-sprinkling ritual.

It felt as if she was outside her body watching the whole spectacle unfold as they passed through the castle's torch-lit corridors to the courtyard where the ceremony would be held. Her dazed gaze swept the magical setting that had become even more so with extensive decorations and ingenious lighting. Alonzo had turned the main building, its satellites and the grounds into a setting for a dream.

They passed through hundreds, maybe thousands, of smiling faces, only a few registering a spark of recognition in her stalled mind. Princes Durante and Eduardo, Gio, Alonzo's partner, and other relatives of Vincenzo's whom she'd met in the past week. Her gaze hiccupped and lingered only once, on her father and brother. They looked so dashing in their fineries, so moved, looking at her so lovingly. Her resentment crumbled and her heart trembled with that affection that had and would always defy logic.

Then Vincenzo swept her away and to the stage that now blocked the doors of the central tower, facing the courtyard where guests milled in concentric semicircles of tables.

As soon as they took the last step up the royal-blue satin-covered stairs, where a sumptuously dressed minister awaited them between King Ferruccio and Crown Prince Leandro, who would be their witnesses, the live medley of regal music stopped. Silence and sea breeze lamented in her ears as Vincenzo handed her down so she could kneel on the velvet cushion before the minister, then he followed her, keeping her molded to his side.

The minister of the province's main church—a jovial man who'd told her how delighted he was to be finally marrying the confirmed bachelor lord of his province—gave a little speech then recited the marriage vows, in Italian then in English, for the bride's guests' benefit. As per Vincenzo's province and family traditions, bride and groom didn't repeat those vows or exchange ones of their own.

She welcomed that. She had nothing to say to Vincenzo. Nothing but the truth of her feelings. And those should not and would never leave her heart to pass through her lips.

Ferruccio came forward with their rings, blessing them

and their union as their king, accepting their bows with that still-pondering smile. This guy was just too astute.

His assessing eyes spiked her agitation so much it made her keep missing Vincenzo's finger as she tried to slip his wedding band on. Vincenzo took hold of her hands and branded them with a kiss that rendered them useless before guiding them through the achingly symbolic ritual. The imaginary pins holding up her smile started to pierce into her flesh.

Then it was Leandro's turn as the second witness to perform the last ritual, coming forward with a crystal goblet. Vincenzo clasped her to his side as he leaned down, plastering his cheek against hers as Leandro held the goblet to their lips for them to simultaneously sip the bloodred liquid that tasted and smelled of an elusive amalgam of spices, fruits and flowers. He recited the words that would "bind their blood" so that they'd never be complete without the other.

Then Vincenzo turned her to face the crowd, who were now on their feet in a standing ovation, holding up their similarly filled glasses and toasting the couple in unison.

This was really happening. She was standing with the man she'd thought she'd lost forever, before his family, friends and followers, before the world, as his bride and princess.

Acting as his bride and princess. *Never forget that, and you might yet survive this.*

Just when she thought the worst was over, Vincenzo made everything infinitely worse.

His magnificent voice rose, carrying on the deepening night's breeze. "My people, my family and friends, everyone blessed to call Castaldini home. I give you your new princess. The glory of my life. Gloria D'Agostino."

If he hadn't had her firmly tucked into his side, she would have folded to the ground.

The canopy of moonlit sky at his back blurred as he looked down at her with an intensity that flayed her already inflamed senses. He brought her back into her body, crushing it to his, and swooped down to claim her lips, reclaiming her wasteland of a soul, feeling like bliss, tasting like life.

The crowd roared its approval accompanied with a storm of clinking glasses as the orchestra played a joyful tune this time, with the majority of the crowd joining in, a song celebrating the newlyweds' future happiness.

As the festivities escalated into the night, she lost herself in the creativity of Alonzo's efforts and the enthusiasm of everyone present. The fantasy of it all deepened until she felt she'd never resurface, until her ordinary, solitary life blipped out from her memory.

Everything became replaced by the wonder of Vincenzo's nearness, by that of his world, and all the wonderful people who populated his life.

And her resolve was resurrected.

Nothing mattered but having this time with Vincenzo. And she would drain every single second of it dry.

Nine

"The ordeal is finally over."

Tremors drenched Glory at Vincenzo's deep purr.

It came from the darkness that enveloped the doorway of her hideaway.

At midnight, as per tradition, Vincenzo's friends had held him back while she'd been "spirited" away by hers. It was supposed to whet the groom's appetites even further, searching for his bride in the castle, until he caught her and carried her back to their marital quarters.

The ladies had deserted her somewhere she'd never been in the castle what felt like an hour ago.

She'd felt like someone in a movie who'd been suddenly left behind somewhere mysterious and otherworldly, filled with whispers of temptation beckoning to an unknown fate.

She'd felt his approach long before she'd heard his voice. She now felt his eyes on her as she stood in the dancing light of a flame-lit brass lantern. Her heart no longer had distinct beats, buzzing like a hummingbird's wings, failing to pump blood to her vitals. The world started to blotch crimson....

His voice brought her jackknifing back to focus. "While being forced to share you with every single person I've known in my life, I've been pretending sanity and civilization for the crowd and the cameras. Now the wait is over."

He appeared as if separating from the darkness, a piece of its endlessness taking the form of the epitome of manhood. The need radiating from him violently strummed her, the reverberations deepening her paralysis.

She could only hurl herself at him, climb him, tear him out of his clothes and devour him in her mind.

Then he was there, against her, pressing her into the wall. Her cry echoed in the almost empty chamber as he ground himself against her. Moans and groans filled her head, high and deep, the sounds of suffering. He was in agony, too. His flesh burned her with his torment.

"Ti voglio tanto...tanto, Gloriosa mia."

Her nod was frantic. "I want you too much, too.... Take me to our room...." She didn't know where that was. Another tradition of the nobility around here. The groom picked the quarters for his bride and prepared them for pampering and pleasuring her. Just imagining it made her plead, *"Please,* Vincenzo...*now."*

He roared as she sank her teeth in his neck to stress her plea. He snatched her off her feet, hurtled with her through the now-deserted winding corridors of his fairy-tale domain.

Doors opened into a place set up like an erotic dream. The vast chamber opened onto a semicircular balcony with wide-open ten-foot doors. The balmy sea breeze wafted in with the scent of jasmine and sandalwood incense, making sheer white curtains dance like gossamer spirits. The flames of a hundred candles undulated like fiery beings. A bed bigger than any she'd thought possible occupied the far end of the room. It was spread in satin the color of her eyes and covered in white and gold rose petals.

But instead of taking her there and putting an end to the torment, he only put her down on her feet.

She stood swaying with the loss of his support and watched him move to stand framed against the moonlit balcony door, her Roman god come to life.

Before she could ask why he'd walked away, his voice cascaded over her, intertwining with the music of the night. "Though I'm dying to end our suffering, there's one thing I want to do first. A wedding night ritual that used to be done here before modernism took over and people started taking too many shortcuts, even in passion. Something I never thought I'd have the chance to do, but always wished I could."

She groaned, louder inwardly. Not another thing to prolong her waiting! "What's that ritual?"

"A striptease. Of sorts."

Okay. Sounded good. Exactly what she wanted to do. Though she wasn't sure her system could withstand watching him strip at this point.

"It has rules, though."

Not so good. He expected her to follow rules, or do anything that required coherence now?

"Would you hurry up and say what those rules are before I liquefy completely?"

His chuckle was pure male pride. "We play a game. The winner gets to dictate the intimacies we share, until the other wins a next one."

"And the rules of the game, dammit?"

His laughter deepened. He loved watching her come apart. "Each says the most audacious thing that has ever crossed their mind about the other, confessing every uninhibited fantasy. According to the enormity of each confession, we shed one or more pieces of clothing."

Now, that wasn't good *at all*. She wasn't ready to expose her most private yearnings.

Which was stupid, when she was begging him to expose *her* to every intimacy he could think of.

But it was one thing for him to do it, for her to revel in having it done to her, another to put her needs into words. She'd been hoping he'd give her what she needed with nothing but surrender on her part, as he'd always done.

But that was exactly what this was about. Making her own her needs heard. Taking pride in them and responsibility for them. An opportunity to be on equal footing with him, at least in this.

And that wasn't bad. Also, she could see he believed he'd win without breaking a sweat, that he would have her writhing in submission before he was through.

He probably would. Didn't mean she'd make it easy for him, or that she would go down without a fight. Dictating intimacies was a hefty prize. Just the idea of having him doing her sensual bidding was worth any risk.

She took the first one. "The first time I saw you, before you ushered me into your office for my interview, you were in your meeting room among all those stuffy suits. All I could think as I shook your hand was whether you tasted as incredible as you smelled. I wanted to know if you looked even more heart-stopping in the throes of pleasure. I wanted to tell the others to get out so I could find out, right there and then. My fantasy went even further, that if they didn't leave, I wouldn't stop, even if it meant giving them a show."

His eyes had darkened with her every word, becoming obsidian pools. His lips belied his eyes' ferocity, spreading wider with approval as he clapped, lazily, sensuously. "I thought you'd balk. Well done."

He took off his sash and slid his cape off his shoulders in an arc, aborting its momentum with a tug that spooled it around his forearm before he let it pool to the ground.

"Taking off pieces of clothing should be simultaneous."

She jerked from her mesmerized gawking, fumbling with her train, almost tearing it off in her haste.

Then it was his turn. "The moment you walked into the room that first day and looked at me with those incredible eyes, I wanted to push you back on my desk, whether anyone remained in my office or not, spread your silky legs and devour you to a screaming orgasm before I even knew who you were."

The fire in her loins was spreading, consuming her, flowing down her thighs. And all he'd done was expose her to his visual and verbal desire and make her confess hers.

He prowled toward her, giving her a hormone-roaring show of contained power and inbred poise as he slipped off his jacket. By the time it thudded to the ground in his wake, she'd torn off her veil, tumbling her chignon in disarray.

"When you showed up on my doorstep that night," she panted, "I thought it would be the first and last time I had you alone. I fantasized about seizing the opportunity, dragging you in, tearing you out of your clothes and losing my mind all over you, even if you fired me for it."

He unbuttoned his shirt, exposing his Herculean torso and abdomen, shrugged the shirt off then yanked off his boots and socks. "All those licentious thoughts when you were a virgin, too."

As she bent to take off her stilettos, a warning finger stopped her. She straightened, swaying in place. "Being a virgin made my fantasies even more licentious. I had no expectations or experience to water them down."

His zipper slid down with a smooth hiss that made her start to shake in earnest.

He let his pants fall then kicked them aside. "Whatever happened to the fantasies after you experienced me?"

Her zipper was undone in a far less assured fashion. Her dress peeled off her swollen breasts under its own weight, sighing in a rustling mass around her ankles. She struggled not to stumble as she stepped out of it.

She stood facing him, in her white lace thong, jewelry and four-inch stilettos, her gaze glued to the erection stretching his boxers.

"They ended." At his frown, she elaborated, "I realized they were actually modest, almost pathetic. You surpassed any fantasy I was creative enough to have."

A shock wave of lust blasted off of him.

Her lips trembled in triumph. "Do I win?"

His chest was heaving now. "All those years, I fantasized about going back for you, dragging you away wherever I found you, taking you somewhere where there was only us, only ever us. I would be in my lab, or in a board meeting or at a summit and I'd sit and plan everything I'd do to you touch by touch. I planned whole nights of arousing you and taking you to the edge again and again until you were begging me to take you over it, to do anything and everything to you, with you. I mapped out the number of orgasms I'd give you, their variations and method before I had mercy on you, took you, rode you until I drained your magnificent body of every spark of sensation it was capable of. Then I planned how to keep you in my power, how to have you beg to be my pleasure slave, and a slave to my pleasure."

"Vincenzo, *pietà*...have mercy now...you win." She stumbled the last steps between them, crushed her breasts against his hard chest, assuaging the pain, accumulating more. "Now dictate. Any intimacy. And just *do* it."

He grabbed her head in both hands. "I always started our intimacies as the hunter, the seeker. Even when you did anything to me, it was at my request, my prodding. But I always fantasized that you'd take the initiative, do anything you want to me. This is what I dictate. That you show me *your* desire, *Gloria mia.*" His hands stabbed into her hair, pulling her away by its tether, demand vehement in his eyes. "Do it."

Vincenzo watched Glory as she pulled away. Her eyes were eclipsed with hunger as she started demonstrating her fantasies.

She touched him all over, explored and owned and worshipped him, in strokes and caresses, in suckles and kisses, in nips and kneads—his chest and abdomen, his arms and hands, his neck and face—telling him how she'd always wanted to do that, every second of every day, how she'd thought nothing, real or imagined, touched him in beauty, in wonder.

He reveled in feeling his mind unravel with her every touch and confession, in feeling her craving cocooning him, claiming him. Then, without warning, she dropped before him, wrapping her arms around his thighs, burrowing her face into his erection.

His eyes glazed over at the sight of her as she knelt before him. The ripe swell of her buttocks, the graceful curve of her back, the gleaming luxury of her hair, her unbridled expression as she drew deep of his feel and scent, as she pulled his boxers down. His engorgement rebounded against his belly, throbbing, straining.

Then she was showing him in glorious sight and sound and touch. And words. Feverish, explicit, uncensored words, confessing all. Exposing the true extent of her desire.

His body hovered on the edge of detonation with every touch, yet plateaued in the most agonizing arousal he'd ever experienced. He felt his life depended on, and was threatened by, prolonging this. His groans merged as her hands owned and explored him, her breath on his flesh a furnace blast, her tongue as it swirled and lapped the flow of his desire a sweep of insanity. Then she engulfed all she could of him, poured delight and delirium all over him. And his mind snapped.

"Enough."

Then she was hauled over his shoulders, gasping and moaning as he hurtled across the room. Her teeth sank into his shoulder blade, unleashing a roar from his depths as he swung her over and down on the bed. He stood back for one more fractured heartbeat, looking down at her, a goddess of abandon and decadence lying open and maddened with need among the petals, her satiny firmness sparkling in his kingdom's treasures, trembling arms outstretched, bidding him come lose his mind. He first rid her of jewels, leaving only the ring, then he lost the last shred of the civilized man and let the beast claw its way out of his skin.

He came down on top of her, yanked her thighs apart and crushed her beneath him. She surged back into him, grinding herself against him, her legs spreading wider, her fingers and nails digging into him, her litany of "don't wait, don't wait, fill me, fill me" completing his descent into oblivion.

Incoherent, he gripped her buttocks, tilted her, bore down on her, then, in one forceful stroke, he plunged inside her, invading her to her recesses. She engulfed him back on a piercing scream, consuming him in her vise of pure molten pleasure.

His bellow rocked him, and her beneath him. *"Glory... at last."*

Her head thrashed, tossing her hair among the petals, her back a steep arch, her voice a pulse of fever. "Yes, Vincenzo, yes...take me, take me back, take all of me..."

But before he did, he rested his forehead on hers, overcome by the enormity of being inside her again. She arched beneath him, taking him all the way to her womb, her eyes streaming, making him feel she'd taken him all the way to her heart like he'd once believed she had.

On a fervent prayer that it was true, he withdrew all the way out of her then thrust back, fierce and full.

Then he rode her. And rode her. To the escalating rhythm of her satin screams, his frenzied rumbles echoing them. It could have been a minute or an hour as the pleasure, the intimacy, rose and deepened. Then, with relief and regret, both of them extreme, he felt his body hurtling to completion. Needing her pleasure first, he held back until her almost unbearable tightness clamped down on his length, pouring a surplus of red-hot welcome over his flesh as she convulsed beneath him, her orgasm tearing through her, wrenching her core around him.

Seeing her lost to the pleasure he'd given her hurled him after her into the abyss of ecstasy. His buttocks convulsed into her cradle as he poured himself inside her, surge after surge of blinding, scorching pleasure. Her convulsions spiked with every splash of his seed, her cries were stifled against his shoulder as she mashed herself into him. He felt her heart boom out of control along with his as the paroxysm of release wiped out existence around them....

"Dio, siete incredibile."

Glory thought this had to be the most wonderful sound in existence. Vincenzo cooing to her. That he was telling her she was incredible didn't hurt, either.

She hadn't slept, not for a second. The first time had also been like that, leaving her with the experience still expanding inside her, awake but in the stasis of stunned satisfaction.

She tried to open her eyes, but they wouldn't cooperate. They were swollen. Just like every inch of her, inside and out. From Vincenzo's ferocious possession, and her fierce response. A numb hand flew to her head, surprised it was still there. He'd almost blown it off with pleasure, discharging the accumulated frustrations and cravings of six years in one annihilating detonation.

And he'd only managed to whet her appetite sharper. She wanted him again, even more than before. Her addiction was fully resurrected and would keep intensifying. Until it ended again.

But now it was just starting. She wanted every second of it before she had to relinquish it all again.

Succeeding in opening her eyes at last, she found him propped over his elbow, draped half over her, his eyes smoldering down at her. "*Dio,* what have you done to yourself? How could you be even more beautiful than before? How could you give me even more pleasure?"

"Look who's talking." She dragged his head down to her, twisting beneath him, bringing him fully on top of her.

He started to kiss her, caress her, but she was too inflamed. She clamped her legs around his waist, thrusting herself against his intact arousal.

He eased her down, unlocked her legs and rose between her splayed thighs, probing her with a finger, then two. Her flesh clamped around their delicious invasion, but it was him she needed inside her. She was flowing for him. He attempted to soothe her frenzy, clearly wanting to take it slower this time. She wouldn't survive slower. Her heartbeats felt as if they'd race each other to a standstill.

"Just take me, Vincenzo," she cried, undulating beneath him, her breasts turgid and aching, her core on fire. "I've needed you inside me for so long…so long…and having you once only made me want more…."

"After six endless years without this, without you, you'll have more, as much as you can survive." He bore her down into the mattress, driving air from her lungs. "Now I take my fill of you. And you take your fill of me. Take it all, *Gloria mia.*"

And he plunged inside her.

Her scream was stifled with that first craved invasion, that elemental feeling of his potency filling her, like a burning dawn, scorching everything away as it spread. He kept plunging deeper, feeling as if he'd never bottom out. Then he did, nudging against what felt like the center of her being. He relented at her scream, resting against the opening of her womb and stilling inside her, overfilling her, inundating her with sensations both agonizing and sublime.

Then the need for him to conquer her rose. Her legs clamped around his back; her heels dug into his buttocks, urging him on; her fractured moans begged for everything, insane for the assuagement of his full power and possession. And he answered, drowning her in a mouth-mating as he drove her beyond ecstasy, beyond her limits, winding that coil of need inside her tighter and tighter with each thrust.

Then he groaned for her to come for him and all the tension spiked and splintered, lashing out through her system in shock waves of excruciating gratification. His tongue filled her, absorbing her cries of pleasure as he filled her with his own, jet after jet of fuel over her fire.

He kissed her all through the descent, rumbling her name again and again, throbbing inside her until the tide receded and cell-deep bliss dragged her into its still, silent realm.

Glory had been awake for a while now.

She kept her eyes closed, regulating her breathing even as her heart stumbled.

From the flickering dimness illuminating her closed lids, she knew it was night again. Twenty-four hours or more had passed since Vincenzo had carried her into this chamber of pleasures. He had said he wasn't coming up for air for at least that long. And he'd kept his promise. How he'd kept it.

After the first two times he'd made love to her, he'd carried her to the adjoining bathroom, an amalgam of old Castaldinian design and cutting-edge luxury. By the time he'd carried her back to bed, he'd melted her into too many orgasms to count. Then they'd spent hours reviving every sensual bond they'd formed years ago. He claimed they'd never loosened their hold over him.

Then he'd let her have him at *her* mercy as she fulfilled her fantasy of losing her mind all over him. Riding him to the most explosive release in her life was the last thing she remembered before waking up minutes ago.

There was a problem, though. She'd woken up so many times, too many, from abandoned nights to feel him wrapped around her like that. Then she'd opened her eyes and he'd dissolved into the emptiness of reality. She was afraid if she opened her eyes now, he might disappear again.

"Gloria mia?"

She'd heard him crooning her name in her waking dreams before. Logically speaking, everything that had culminated in their wedding night had to be some lovelorn hallucination....

Every nerve in her body fired in unison as the hand cupping her breast started caressing it to the fullness of need again.

Okay. None of her tormenting phantasms had felt that real. That good. That meant that even if it made no sense whatsoever, Vincenzo *was* really wrapped around her after a night of magic beyond her wildest fantasies.

Then his silk-covered leg drove between hers, pressing just where she needed. He must have sensed she was awake. Or her heart must have been shaking the whole bed.

No use pretending to be asleep now.

She opened her eyes. The best sight in existence filled her

vision. Vincenzo. His every line thrown into relief by stark shadows and the illumination of the gibbous moon pouring from the open window. But it was his expression that had her on the verge of crushing herself against him and weeping.

She must be seeing what she longed to see. Or she was superimposing what *she* felt on him. He couldn't be looking at her as if he couldn't believe she was in his arms again. As if he was afraid to blink and miss one nuance of her, one second with her. As if he loved her. As if he'd always loved her.

As if responding to her need to escape the impossible yearnings, his expression shifted to another kind of passion as he weighed and kneaded her breast. "I think I will fulfill my fantasy, after all. I'll keep you here as my pleasure slave." She moaned, arched, pressed her breast harder into his big palm. Something elemental rumbled in his gut. "The way you respond to my every word and touch is pure magic. What you do to me by just existing is beyond even that."

Her hips moved to yield to the erection that she was still stunned she could accommodate. Her moan grew louder as he expanded and hardened even more. "It's only fair that I turn you inside out like you do me."

Indulgence smoldered in his eyes. "So we're even."

"*Not* unless we play musical slaves."

"After what you did to me last night, I might cheat and let you sit on the chair every time. I'll let you sit anywhere you want, as many times and as long as you want."

"Oh, I want. I *want,* Vincenzo."

Unable to bear the emptiness inside her that only he could fill, she tried to drag him over and inside her. He resisted her, slid down her body, looking up as she twisted in his hold.

"I have a six-year hunger that I need to appease, *gloriosa mia.* Surrender to me, let me take my fill."

And she collapsed, could do nothing but submit to his will and let him take everything he wanted, let him drive her to madness, over and over until he'd drained her dry of reason. Of worries. Of anything that wasn't him.

When next she woke, it was night again, and she was alone.

Before dismay could register, the door creaked open and in Vincenzo walked with a huge, piled tray in his hands. In a molded gray shirt and pants, he looked like a god come down to earth to mess with mortals' wills and jeopardize their souls.

His smile was indulgence itself as he put the tray aside to pull her up to a sitting position. The sheet fell off, exposing her breasts. As if he couldn't help it, he bent and saluted each nipple with soft pulls, soothing the soreness she'd literally pummeled him to inflict on her.

He pulled back reluctantly. "No more temptation, princess." He chuckled at her pout. "I'd do nothing but service and pleasure Your Royal Voluptuousness nonstop, but I have to refuel you so you can withstand the week ahead."

She sighed her pleasure as she sifted her fingers through the thick, silky depths of his hair. "I've been holding up pretty well for the past two days. What's so different about the week ahead?"

"First, for the past two days you haven't even left this room. You have been mostly flat on your back—or belly—and apart from a couple of memorable instances, I've been doing all the work." She smacked him playfully, giggling, her body priming itself again at the memory of all the "work" he'd done. "But I'm going to demand more of your participation over the next week, as it's all the time I have for our honeymoon. My post back in New York starts next week."

Her heart plummeted. That soon?

She must have looked as crestfallen as she felt. He smoothed her tousled bangs out of her eyes, his tone urgent. "I'll only work by day. The nights, I'm all yours."

She smiled, hating that she'd made him feel bad for having to work. "It's okay. I need to get back to work myself."

His eyes flared with possessiveness as he slid the sheet totally off her. "During the days only, *Gloriosa mia*. The nights are mine."

She nodded dreamily as she squeezed her breasts and thighs together to mitigate their aching throb. "Yes."

His eyes glazed over as he pushed her thighs apart, sliding two fingers between her soaked folds. "And afternoons and lunch breaks and whenever I can squeeze you in."

Her legs fell apart, inviting his fingers inside; her breasts jutted for him to squeeze away. "Oh, yes."

Her response tore away any intentions to prioritize food as he fell on her breasts again, suckling, his fingers plunging inside her, pumping. She poured fuel on his fervor, kneading his erection, sinking her teeth into his shoulders.

"*Dio, Gloria mia,* you make me insane…."

His growl was driven as he descended over her, pushed her flat on her back, impacting her with his full weight and rising between her spread legs only enough to free himself.

Then, without preliminaries, he drove into her, tearing a shriek from her depths. He rammed inside her in a furious rhythm, plunging deeper with every thrust, growling like a beast. The expansion inside her around his girth and length, the feeling of being totally dominated and mastered, had her sobbing, pleasure twisting tighter inside her until she feared she'd unravel once it snapped.

He rose on outstretched arms. "Look at us, *Gloria mia,* look what I'm doing to you, look how you're taking me…."

She looked, and the sight of the daunting column of flesh disappearing inside her, spreading her, joining them, made her thrash at the carnality of it, the beauty.

Then the tightness was quickening inside her, the familiar crescendo, her flesh fluttering around his girth.

He felt it, fell on her breasts, suckling hard, biting, triggering her. "Come for me, *gloriosa,* come all over me. Finish me with your pleasure as I finish you."

Everything snapped inside her like a high-voltage cable, writhing and lashing out and wreaking devastation. He drove the deepest he'd ever been inside her, roaring as he rested against her womb and razed her in the ecstasy of his release.

But feeling his seed splashing her intimate walls, filling her, branding her, spread regret along with the pleasure. Regret that his seed wouldn't take root. She'd made sure it wouldn't.

He collapsed on top of her, his breathing as harsh as hers. She wrapped herself tighter around him, relishing his weight. Without him covering her like this, anchoring her in the aftermath of devastation, she felt she might dissipate....

He drew up, supporting his weight on one elbow, fusing them in the evidence of their mutual satisfaction, his other hand securing her head for a deep, luxurious kiss.

The moment he felt her quickening beneath him again, he rumbled a self-deprecating laugh, then groaned as he separated their bodies. "Have mercy, *bellissima.* Now it's I who needs to refuel. I'm not a spry teenager anymore."

Her gaze clung to his undiminished manhood. "Are you kidding me? I've been wondering if you've hooked yourself to your inexhaustible energy source."

"I am hooked, all right, on a perpetually renewable source of passionate madness whose name is but a description of her." Before she could lunge at him, he jumped up, stuffing himself with difficulty into his pants. "*We're* refueling. Then I'm taking you sailing. We'll continue this session on board. Ever made love rocking to the undulations of a tranquil sea?"

Before she said no, since he hadn't taken her sailing before, jealousy sank into her gut.

He grinned. "Neither have I. Another fantasy I'll fulfill.

I wrote a list of one hundred and ten items while you slept. I intend to make serious headway into all of them during the next week."

Her tension deflated. He hadn't done it before. He hadn't done so many things, but he wanted to do them all with her. Because she was the only one who made him want them. Just like he was the only one who made her want everything and anything.

She arched sensuously, smoothing her hands down her breasts, her tummy, delighting in the soreness inside and out. "I thought we were going to take turns playing out fantasies."

He tugged her up by the hand, this time making sure not to come too close and be snared back. "*Incantatrice mia,* I just played one of yours now. Taking you with no foreplay, just rough domination and explosive satisfaction."

So he could read her like a hundred-foot billboard.

He brought back the tray, placed it across her thighs and bent for one last kiss before he withdrew quickly, making her bite him in her effort to cling.

He laved her bite with a wince of enjoyment. "Eat something else for now, *amore mio.* I have to go prepare the rest of the day, then the week. I promise your fantasies are going to be heavily featured and meticulously taken care of."

With one last wink, he turned and strode out.

She watched him go, everything on pause.

Had he said *amore mio?*

My love?

Ten

Amore mio.

The words rang in a loop inside Glory's head as she stood staring around her condo. *Amore mio, amore mio*—crooned in Vincenzo's voice, soaked in his passion.

He'd been calling her that constantly, among all the other endearments he kept lavishing on her. At least he had for the first six weeks after their wedding. It had been over a week now that he hadn't been around to call her much of anything.

They'd been back to New York after their honeymoon ended. Vincenzo had extended their time away to two weeks at a hefty cost to all the people who'd arranged their schedules counting on his presence a week earlier.

A wave of oppression descended over her as images from those two weeks in paradise bombarded her. At their end, she'd thought that if she died then, she would have certainly died the most fulfilled, pleasured and pampered woman on earth.

Then they'd gone back to New York. He'd started his position and she'd gone back to work, and instead of everything slowing and cooling down, it had gotten better, hotter. He'd kept his promises and more, making time for her, for them, always, but even better, making a place for her in his working life, and asking for and taking a place in hers.

He'd taken her with him to every function, showing her off as if she was his most vital asset. He'd come to her like he used to with his work issues, taking her opinion and following her advice. He'd thrown his full weight into making difficulties in her work disappear and making far-fetched hopes achievable, without her even asking.

And through it all he'd been saying *amore mio*. My love.

He'd called her that in the past. She'd believed he'd meant it. Then everything had happened, and she'd known the name had just been an empty endearment. Now, she no longer knew what to believe. After he'd confessed he'd lied about his reasons for leaving her. After the past weeks in his arms, in his life.

So what had it meant to him then? What did it mean now?

The need to ask, to understand everything that had happened in the past, mushroomed daily. She'd tried more than once to broach the subject, but he'd always diverted her, unwilling to talk about it, as if he hated to bring up the past, fearing it would taint the present.

She could understand that. He appeared to have decided to live in the moment, without consideration for the past or the future. And she tried to do that, too, succeeding most of the time. At least, when he was with her. The moment she was out of his orbit, obsessions attacked her, and questions that had never been answered preyed on her. And it was all because she'd done an unforgivable thing.

She'd let herself hope. That this wouldn't be temporary, that it couldn't be, not when it was so incredible.

At least it had been incredible until last week when he'd suddenly started becoming unavailable. Even though he'd apologized, blamed work problems, swore it would only be temporary, his absence had plunged her into a nightmarish déjà vu. Though he still came home, still made love to her—not like before when he'd cut her off suddenly—it still made her feel this was the beginning of the end. She tried to tell herself that the "honeymoon" was over, that it happened with everyone, that there was no way he could have sustained that level of intensity. It didn't mean anything was wrong.

Tell that to her glued-back-together heart.

But all her upheaval had one origin. The missing piece that could explain how the noble man she was now certain Vincenzo was could have been so cruel to her.

Her eyes fell on the prenup he'd left on her entrance cabinet what felt like ages ago, and something turned in her head, clicked.

Her eyes jerked up, slamming into their reflection in the mirror above as that missing piece crashed into place.

Her family.

God, how hadn't it occurred to her before? This had to be the explanation. He'd said her father and Daniel had been perpetrating crimes for a long time. What if it had been as far back as six years, and he'd discovered it when he'd been investigating them during his espionage crisis?

Then another idea whacked her like an uppercut.

Even if he'd found it out of the question to be involved with someone with a family of criminals, there had been no reason to be vicious with her over her family's crimes. That meant one thing. He'd thought she'd been involved in those crimes. Or worse, he'd thought she'd embezzle or defraud him, too, and had thought to preempt her, cut her off before she had the chance.

Gasping as suspicions solidified into conviction, she staggered to the nearest horizontal surface, sitting heavily.

Then another realization pushed aside the debris of shame and anguish.

He'd believed her an accomplice to her family, a danger to him, and he'd simply walked away. He'd turned vicious only when she'd cornered him. That meant one thing—he *had* felt something for her. Something strong enough that it stopped him from prosecuting her even when he'd thought she deserved it.

Following that same rationalization, the way he was with her now, even with his new evidence of her family's crimes, meant that he believed she couldn't be party to those. As for what she'd been seeing in his eyes, the way he said *amore mio,* this could mean…

In the next moment her trembling hope was shot down like a bird before it could spread its wings.

Even if he didn't think she was involved in illegal activities now, he would never think her worth more than a fleeting place in his life. And who could blame him?

She couldn't.

Her aching eyes panned around her condo. She'd come here to empty it, to end its lease. Vincenzo had asked her to do so a couple of weeks ago. She'd felt alarmed at what that implied and had groped for a reason to dismiss his request, arguing she needed a place to entertain family and friends away from their own private quarters. But he'd already thought of that, producing a lease to another condo, far more lavish, and a minute's walk from his building. It looked as if he was thinking of her all the time, going out of his way to provide her with anything that would make her life easier, fuller.

But she couldn't count on anything from him, or with him. She wouldn't do this to herself again. She had to live with the expectation that this would end, and after last week, it appeared that the end would be sooner rather than later. She had to be ready to fade back into her own life once he pulled away completely. But to do that, she had to make sure she had a life to fade back to.

She rose, headed back to the suitcases she'd packed, opened them and started putting everything back in its place.

An hour later, on her way out, she stopped by the entrance cabinet. After a long moment of staring at the prenup, she picked it up.

Vincenzo whistled an upbeat tune as he exited the shower.

He caught his eyes in the steamed-up mirror and grinned widely at himself. He felt like whistling all the time now. Or singing. He'd been struggling not to do either in all those stuffy meetings and negotiations he'd been attending. He'd had the most important one so far today, what he'd been working toward since he'd gone back to New York with Glory after their honeymoon six weeks ago.

The memory of their honeymoon cascaded through him again. He'd extended it for a week and had representatives of a dozen countries scrambling to readjust their schedules. When they'd complained, he'd told them they instead had to thank his bride for putting their agendas ahead of her rights and consenting to cut short her honeymoon for them. He'd seen to it that each and every one *had* thanked her, in all the functions to which she'd accompanied him.

A thrill of pride spread through him. She'd been beyond magnificent. A consort of a caliber he couldn't have dreamed of. Though she'd gone back to her own hectic schedule, she always made time for him. She aided, guided and supported him with her counsel, honored, soothed and delighted him with her company. Every moment with her, in and out of bed, had been better than anything he'd dared plan or hope for.

He'd never known happiness like this existed.

Just as he thought that, a frown invaded his elation.

He hadn't been able to have her with him for over two weeks now. With back-to-back meetings and unending follow-up work, he'd had to leave her behind, cancel dates and generally have no time for her. He hadn't even come home for the past three days.

He was paying the price for taking too much time with her during the first weeks of their marriage. Work had accumulated until it had become unmanageable, and resolving the mess had been like digging in the sea, with new chores only pouring over the unfinished ones. He'd needed to clean out his agenda then start fresh using the system Glory had set up for him.

So, for the past two weeks, he'd worked flat out to get this phase, the groundwork his whole mission was built on, out of the way once and for all.

Though it had been agonizing being without her, at least he'd succeeded in fixing the problem he'd caused by being too greedy for her. He was now out of the bottleneck and the first phase of his mission here had been concluded.

And before he entered the next phase, he had a prolonged vacation with Glory planned. A second honeymoon. He intended to have another one every month.

Grinning to himself again, luxuriating in the anticipation, he entered the office he hadn't used for weeks.

He saw it the moment he stepped inside and recognized it for what it was at once.

The prenup agreement.

Was his mind playing tricks on him? He'd left it in Glory's condo over two months ago.

A surge of trepidation came over him as he neared it, approaching it as if it was a live grenade. A quick, compulsive check ended any doubt. That *was* the copy he'd given her.

Why was it on his desk, as if Glory was loath to hand it

to him face-to-face? If she was, why put it there at all? After all this time? All this intimacy?

What was she trying to tell him?

Was she reinforcing his original conditions, telling him this was still how she viewed their marriage? As a temporary hostile takeover? But that had stopped being true almost from the start. He'd told her he'd changed his mind after *hours* of being with her again. She hadn't changed her mind after weeks of being with him? But she'd agreed to marry him of her free will, then proceeded to blow his mind with passion and pleasure ever since. He'd thought she'd been showing him that she'd forgotten how this had started, that she'd been demonstrating with actions how she now viewed their relationship, that she wanted it to continue. He sat down, staring at the offensive volume as if it was his worst mistake come back to haunt him. Which it was.

And it was his fault it was haunting him. He'd avoided a confrontation about the past, with her, with himself. He'd just been so scared it might spoil the perfection they had now.

But here was what avoidance had led to.

He now had to admit to himself what he'd been thinking and feeling all along.

He'd at first thought she'd changed her ways. But when he couldn't find a trace of subterfuge in her—something that couldn't be wiped so totally from someone's character—he'd been able to sanction only one thing. That she'd always been what he'd believed her to be from the start, the upstanding human being and the incredible woman he'd fallen in love with. And this had led him to one conclusion. That she'd been forced into her past betrayal.

There was only one scenario that made sense. As soon as he'd employed her, those who always looked for chinks in his armor got to her family, and through them, to her. Younger, vulnerable to her family's needs, she'd been forced to do their bidding, probably under fear of losing them to imprisonment through their crippling debts. That *had* been the first thing that had occurred to her when *he'd* threatened to imprison them.

But she must have hated doing it and soon realized there'd been no excuse for what they'd forced her to do. She *had* struck out as far away from them as possible, becoming the magnificent force for good she was now.

But after observing her with her family, with her mother especially, he was now certain Glory had no idea that he'd discovered her betrayal, or she would have understood why he'd kicked her out of his life. Her mother clearly hadn't told her of the climactic confrontations with him. Probably out of shame that she'd exposed her daughter to buy the rest of her family's salvation.

Or he might be all wrong and there might be another explanation. But whatever it was, he was certain she hadn't set him up in cold blood, or pretended emotions she hadn't felt. Everything in him just *knew* that her involvement with him had been real, and predated whatever she'd been forced to do. And that was the one thing that mattered to him.

Where he was concerned, from the moment he'd told her she was free not to marry him, that past had been wiped out from his mind and heart. Nothing remained in him now but that he wanted her, *loved* her, far more than he ever had.

But it was clear she had no idea this was how he felt. This must be why she was offering him the prenup. Showing him that he was free to keep his original pact if he wanted.

It was time to make a full admission, to leave her in no doubt what he wanted. Her. As his wife, for real and forever.

He heaved up to his feet, excitement frothing inside him, and swiped the prenup off the desk.

He'd take that piece of paranoid crap he'd regretted ever since it had passed from his hands to hers and tear it to pieces. He'd throw it at her feet along with his heart and his life. He'd…

His phone rang.

Gritting his teeth at the interruption, he answered the call. A moment later, he wished he hadn't.

A deep, somber voice poured into his ear, and everything inside him tightened, as if to ward off a blow.

Now what?

"Thanks for seeing me on such short notice, Prince Vincenzo."

Vincenzo's unease rose. Brandon Steele never asked to see him unless there was some catastrophe brewing.

"We're alone now so drop the titles, please, Brandon."

The man inclined his head silently, looking, as always, like a strange cross between a suave celebrity and a linebacker. He had a quietly menacing aura hanging over him like a cloak.

Vincenzo had hired him seven years ago to protect his research and businesses against sabotage and intellectual property theft. The agency Brandon owned and ran, Steele Security, had come highly recommended by Vincenzo's cousin Eduardo as the most effective undercover agency to handle financial fraud and industrial espionage.

Brandon held a spotless track record, had uncovered dozens of masterful infiltrations and conspiracies, saved Vincenzo and his cousins untold millions and smoothed the course of their rise to the top of their respective fields.

But it was one particular achievement that always made Vincenzo loath to see him, more now than ever.

He'd been the one who'd gotten proof of Glory's espionage six years ago.

Getting to the point as always, Brandon exhaled. "I don't know how to say this, Vincenzo, but what were you thinking? You married the woman who once spied on you?"

Was that it? Brandon was here to scold him?

"Things aren't as simple as they look to you, Brandon."

Brandon cocked one disbelieving eyebrow. "Aren't they?"

Vincenzo had no time for skepticism. If not for Brandon's untimely call, he could have been with Glory right now, resolving everything with her.

Vincenzo exhaled. "Did you detect another leak in my operations? And you jumped to the conclusion that the only new thing in my life is Glory, again, so she must be involved somehow?"

Brandon stared at him as if he'd grown a third eye. "I see you're not concerned about the prospect of a leak."

It was strange, but he wasn't. Or if he was, it was only mentally, for all logical reasons and considerations. But there was no trace of the all-out agitation and anger he'd once experienced, when his work had been the central thing in his life. His priorities *had* changed irrevocably. They all revolved around Glory now.

He sighed. "I thought your security system was now impenetrable."

Brandon gave a curt nod. "It is. And there is no leak."

"So you just want to reprimand me for marrying Glory? You don't know much about who she is now if you're even worried."

Brandon gave him a long-suffering look. "It's my business to know everything about everyone. I know exactly who she is and what she does. The body of work she's amassed over the past five years is nothing short of phenomenal."

He exhaled. "Just spit out the 'but' you're here to say."

"*But* I think this might be a far more elaborate facade than the one she had six years ago."

He waved the man's words away. "I don't care about the past anymore, Brandon."

"I'm not talking about the past."

Everything inside Vincenzo hit pause. "You just said there's been no leak."

"Not in *your* operations, no. But you are deep in negotiations with multinational interests on behalf of Castaldini. I caught leaks of vital info that only you could know, that could end up costing Castaldini the projects and investments you're on the verge of securing on its behalf."

Vincenzo's temperature started to rise, his muscles turning to stone. "The sides I'm negotiating with are privy to the same info, and the leak could be on their side."

"It isn't."

At the curt final statement, he found himself on his feet, agitation no longer in check. "Why on earth are you suspecting Glory when she had no part in any of this?"

"You mean she isn't privy to the details of your dealings and the innermost workings of your mind this time around?"

He shook his head, felt his brain clanging against his skull. "No—I mean, I *do* consult with her—you know there's no one better than her when it comes to negotiations—and she has been advising me, and I've used every shred of advice she gave me to my advantage, but that doesn't mean she—"

Brandon interrupted his ramblings. "*Do* you observe all the security measures I devised in your shared space?"

Vincenzo hadn't even given security a thought around her. But... "*No.* Stop right there. This isn't Glory's doing. I'm certain. Whatever happened in the past, it must have been against her will. She's worked so hard ever since to make good, to turn her life around. With only the power of her benevolence and perseverance she's done more for more people than I've done with all my power and money. I'm never suspecting her again."

Brandon gave him the look of a disapproving parent. "May I remind you it wasn't 'suspicion' last time? I gave you proof, proof you yourself verified, from her closest people."

Vincenzo's voice rose, no longer under his control. "I *told* you the past has nothing to do with the present. And then it turned out she actually saved me from making the worst mistake of my life."

"So you should forgive someone because she didn't succeed in killing you, but inadvertently made you jump and save yourself from falling into a pit? How far are you willing to stretch to make excuses for her, Vincenzo?"

"As far as I need to. When all is said and done, I'm in a much better place now and it is because of what happened."

"Even if it turns out for the best, a failed attempt at a crime still deserves punishment."

"And I *did* punish her," he bellowed. "I passed sentence on her without a trial, without even giving her the chance to defend herself. And what did all that righteousness get me? Six years of hell, without her. Now I have her back, and I'm never losing her again."

Brandon gaped at him for a long, long moment.

Then he grimaced. "God, this is worse than I thought. You're totally under her spell."

"I *love* her."

"And she betrayed you again. What a mess."

Vincenzo barely held back from punching him. "Stop saying that and look elsewhere, Brandon. You're not infallible, remember? You made a mistake with Eduardo's wife."

"It wasn't a mistake. Jade *was* hacking into his system."

"Under duress," he gritted out. "And she was doing that in order to fortify it, so no one could infiltrate it again. As I said, everything isn't always as it seems. You were right, but you were also wrong. You're wrong again now. I don't only love Glory, I *know* her."

Brandon pinned him with a conflicted gaze before he finally squared his shoulders and held out the dossier he had with him. It had the Steele Security insignia on it. Vincenzo knew from experience those were only used for final reports and verified evidence.

Trepidation overwhelmed Vincenzo as he looked at it. He snatched his gaze back to Brandon's, as if to escape an image that would sear his retinas if he gazed at it a second more.

Brandon looked at him like someone would look at a patient before amputating a limb. "I can't tell you how sorry I am, Vincenzo, but this is a compilation of all emails and text messages leaking the info. The originating addresses were expertly hidden, just not expertly enough to hide them from me. Everything was traced back to Glory's phone and computer."

Eleven

Vincenzo had no idea what he'd said to Brandon or when the man had left.

He found himself sitting in the bedroom he had only ever used with Glory. He'd bought this place six years ago when she'd consented to be his. He'd left it when he sent her away, but hadn't been able to sell it off. He'd only come back when he'd decided to have her back in his life.

The life that was falling apart all over again.

This couldn't be happening. Not again.

And he refused to believe it was. There had to be some explanation other than the obvious, other than what Brandon sanctioned. But Vincenzo couldn't think what it was. So he wouldn't even try to think. He'd stop everything, his very heartbeat if need be, until she told him what to think.

He sat there for what might have been hours until he heard her coming into the penthouse. The sense of déjà vu almost overwhelmed him, of that day more than six years ago when he'd waited for her in this room, listening to her advance and feeling that every step was inching toward the end of everything worth living for.

Then she entered the room. For the moment she didn't notice him as he sat to her far right on the couch by the floor-to-ceiling windows, her expression was subdued, pensive. Suddenly she started, her head jerking around, as if his presence electrified her.

Her uncensored reaction the split second she saw him was a smile that felt like a flare of light and warmth in the cold darkness that was spreading inside him.

Her rush toward him felt as if life itself was rushing back into his veins. Her eagerness flooded him, submerged him as she straddled him on the couch.

He let her deluge him in her sweetness, drink him dry in the desperation of her need.

Her kisses grew wrenching, her gasps labored. "I missed you…missed you, darling…Vincenzo…"

And how he'd missed her. Three days and nights without losing himself in the depths of her and drinking deep of her pleasures had him raving mad with starvation.

Her hands fumbled with his clothes, and he knew. The moment she touched his flesh he'd go up in flames, and he owed it to her to settle this before he let her drag him into their realm of delirium. His hands covered hers, stopping her.

She stiffened. Then slowly, as if afraid something would shatter if she moved too fast, she took her lips away from his neck. After a harsh intake of breath, she turned her head away and her rigidity increased as her gaze fixed on a spot on the couch. The security report file lay close to him. He knew she'd recognize it for what it was. But her gaze was fixed farther away, on the prenup.

She spilled off him, staggering up only to take two steps before slumping down on the opposite armchair. She looked at him as if waiting for a blow.

He had to hear her reasons from her own lips. "Why did you put this on my desk today, Glory?"

"Today?" Her eyes rounded. "I—I put it there over a week ago. I thought you'd long seen it, and when you didn't mention it I thought..."

"What did you think?"

A spasm seized her face. "I didn't know what to think."

"What did you want me to think when I saw it? What were you telling me?"

The pained look deepened; her voice sounded strangled. "I was offering you my answer to what I thought you were telling me, when you... When you..."

"When I what?"

"When you stopped taking me to your functions and started canceling our dates."

"What did you think I was telling you?"

"What you said when you didn't come ho...here the past three nights. What you just said very clearly. That this time around it took much less than six months for you to get tired of me."

Her lips, her chin, shook on the last words. The tethers of his heart shook, almost tearing themselves out.

"But then I expected that from the beginning," she choked out. "And now that I realize what you think happened in the past, I'm even wondering why you wanted me again at all. This is why I brought you the prenup, since I thought you must have been regretting not taking it, must be worried about repercussions with no provisions in place when you ended it with me again. But it's a good thing I didn't let my condo go as you told me to. I'll move back there tonight."

"Glory…"

She spoke over his plea, as if hearing his voice hurt her. "I will pretend we're still together so no one will know anything before you're ready to announce our split when the year is over. Until then, whenever you need me to make appearances with you, y-you have my number. If I'm not traveling, I'll play the part I agreed to."

And he was on his feet, then at hers, his hands going around her beloved head, making her raise her wounded gaze to his. "Every single thing you thought has no basis in fact. I didn't get tired of you. I would sooner get tired of breathing."

Redness surged in her eyes, her whole face shaking. "D-don't say that…don't say what you don't mean. Not again."

"The only time I said what I didn't mean to you was that day I kicked you out of my life. I did… I *do* love you, I never loved anyone but you, never had anyone since you."

Her eyes seemed to melt, her cheeks flooding with tears. "Oh, God, Vincenzo…I can't… I don't…"

"You have to believe me." He aborted her headshake, pulling her into a fierce kiss, before drawing away to probe her stunned face. "But you said you now realized what I thought in the past. You mean you now know why I left you?"

Her nod was difficult. "You knew about my family's crimes—thought me their accomplice?"

"It was much worse than that."

Her eyes flew wider. "What *could* be worse?"

And he finally confessed. Everything. Everything but the latest blow Brandon had dealt him.

By the time he'd fallen silent, she was frozen. Even her tears had stopped midway down her cheeks. She wasn't breathing.

It felt like an hour later when she finally choked out, "Your research *was* stolen and my…*mother* told you…told you…"

The rest backlashed in her throat, seeming to go down as if it was broken glass. Anguish so fierce gripped her every feature, radiated from her, buffeting him.

"I now believe that they must have forced you…or something…I just know it wasn't your fault. Just like I believe this latest security breach can't be your doing."

Her wounded eyes widened. "What latest security breach?"

Feeling as if he was spitting razors, he said, "Top secret data in my current negotiations have been leaked. According to this security report I got today, the leak came from your phone and computer."

She jerked as if he'd shot her.

He grabbed her shoulders, begging. "I can't think anymore, Glory, and I won't. I want you to tell me what to think. Trust me, please, tell me everything and I will solve it all. I'm on your side this time, and only on your side, and will always be, no matter what…."

She started shaking her head, her hands gripping it as if to keep it from bursting.

"*Amore, per favore,* please, believe me, let me help…."

Her incoherent cry cut him off as she exploded to her feet. Before another nerve fired, she'd hurtled out of the bedroom and slammed out of the penthouse.

By the time he ran after her, she was gone.

Glory stared at the woman she thought loved her beyond life itself. The woman whose betrayal had wrecked her life.

Her mother's silent tears poured down her cheeks, her eyes pleading.

For what? Glory's understanding? Her forgiveness? How could she give either when there was nothing left inside her? Everything had been destroyed. Nothing was left but shock and disillusionment. They expanded from her gut, threatening to burst her arteries, her heart. They crashed through her in torrents of decimating agony.

"You have to know the rest, darling," her mother choked out.

There was more? She couldn't hear any more. She had to get out of here, hide, disappear.

She escaped her mother's imploring hands as she ran again. She never wanted to stop running.

She spilled out into the street, ran and ran.

But there was no outrunning the realizations.

Everything was far worse than her worst projections. But one thing was worse than anything else. One realization.

Vincenzo's cruelty to her perceived betrayal hadn't been cruel at all. Cruel would have been to have her arrested. Even that would have only been his right, what he should have done. But he hadn't. That meant one thing.

He *had* loved her.

He'd loved her so much that even getting incontrovertible proof of her betrayal hadn't made him retaliate. He'd only tried to protect himself, cutting her off. Then, when she wouldn't let him, he'd pushed her away in a way he'd thought wouldn't harm her, since he'd believed she'd felt nothing for him, had been manipulating him from day one.

And she'd always thought getting answers would resolve the misery that had consumed six years of her life. In truth, it had dealt her a fatal blow.

Despair and exertion hacked through her lungs as more details and realizations sank their shards into her heart…

"Glory."

Vincenzo. His booming desperation shattered everything inside her into shrapnel of grief, of panic. It all burst out into a surge of manic speed.

She couldn't stop. Couldn't let him catch her.

Not now that she knew he'd always loved her. Now that she knew it could never be.

* * *

Vincenzo arrived at the Monaghans' house just as Glory exited it. It was clear the confrontation with her mother had devastated her.

A man in his right mind would have caught up with her without alerting her. But the mass of desperation that he'd turned into had just bellowed her name the moment he'd seen her, sending her zooming faster, screeching for a cab.

But he could have overtaken a speeding car right now. A woman running in high heels looked stationary compared to his speed. He intercepted her as she opened the cab's door.

His arms went around her, filling them with his every reason for living. "Glory, *amore,* please, let's talk."

She pushed weakly at him. "There's nothing more to talk about, Vincenzo. Just forget I ever existed. In fact, when your situation allows, just prosecute me and my family."

Before he could utter another word, she surprised him by ducking out of the circle of his arms and into the cab.

His first instinct was to haul her out, carry her back to their home and tell her he'd never let her go again.

The one thing that stopped him was knowing it would be pointless without performing another imperative step first. Another confrontation with her mother. He had to break whatever hold she had on Glory, once and for all.

After Glory's cab disappeared, with his every cell rioting, he turned and walked back to the Monaghans' house.

The woman who opened the door exhibited Glory's same devastation. He wanted to blast her off the face of the earth for what she'd cost him and Glory, but he couldn't. She looked so fragile, so desolate, so much like an older version of Glory, that he couldn't hate her. He even felt a tug of unreasoning affection.

She grabbed at him with weak, shaking hands. "Glory wouldn't listen to me, but please, Vincenzo, you have to."

Suddenly, looking into those eyes that could be Glory's, everything fell into place.

It had never been Glory. It had always been Glenda.

He staggered under the blow of realization. How had he never considered this?

"It was you. In the past, and again now."

The woman's tears ran thicker, her whole face working. "I—I did it to save Dermot and Daniel!"

Her sob tore through him, with its agony, its authenticity. So he'd been right, just about the wrong person. Glenda Monaghan had been the one who'd been forced to spy on him.

She was now weeping so hard he feared she might tear something vital inside her.

His arm went around her as she swayed, helping her to the nearest couch. He sat beside her, rubbing her shaking hands soothingly. "Mrs. Monaghan, please, calm down. I'm not angry this time, and I promise, I won't hurt you or them. Just tell me why you did it, let me help."

"No one can help," she wailed.

He forced a tight smile. "You clearly don't realize what kind of power your son-in-law has. I would turn the whole world upside down for Glory, and by extension for her family."

"You're a scientist and a prince. You can't possibly know how to handle those...those monsters."

"Who do you mean?"

"The mob!"

And he'd thought nothing could ever surprise him again.

He raised his hands as if to brace against more blows. "Just tell me everything from the beginning."

She nodded, causing her tears to splash on his hands. It made him hug her tighter, trying to absorb her upheaval.

Then haltingly, tearfully, she began. "Fifteen years ago, I was diagnosed with lymphoma. Dermot panicked because our insurance would pay only for a tiny percentage of my treatments, and we were already in debt. At the time, Dermot and I worked in a huge multinational corporation, him in accounting, me in IT. Our financial troubles were soon common knowledge and a guy from work approached Dermot with a way to make easy, serious money."

She paused to draw a long, shaky breath.

"Dermot told me and I refused. But I was soon in no condition to work and with only one income and the bills piling up, it was soon untenable. Dermot began to gamble then fix books and was soon so deep in debts and trouble that when the recruiter approached him again, he agreed.

"For a while, I was so tired and drained, I was just relieved we weren't scrabbling anymore. I bought his stories that he'd entered a partnership in a thriving import/export operation. Then things started getting uglier with his mob bosses asking terrible things of him. And the worst part was they'd also dragged Daniel, who was only nineteen, into their dirty business.

"Unable to go on, Dermot had us pack everything and move across the country. We kept hopping from one place to another in his efforts to escape the mob. During remissions, I worked from home, but my relapses kept draining us. Dermot and Daniel kept trying everything to keep us afloat. But at least the mob was off our back. After seven years, I thought we were home free.

"Then six years ago, I got a call. The man said that they'd always wanted *me,* the real expert in the family, and that they had some jobs for me, if I valued my husband's and son's lives. They owned us. Not only with the debts but with what they had on them. They'd send them to prison if I didn't cooperate." Shame twisted in his gut, that he'd once employed the same method with Glory. "But it wouldn't end with prison if I said no. Accidents happened on the inside, even easier than on the outside. The job was you. They'd found out about your relationship with Glory and thought it put me in a perfect position to spy on you."

He stared at her, six years worth of agony being rewritten, the realization of the needless loss of his life with Glory choking him up.

Glenda sobbed harder now. "As a taste of what they'd do if I refused, they beat Daniel up—we told Glory it was a bar fight—and he was hospitalized for a month. I was ready to do anything after that. And I did. I used Glory's total trust in me, and your total trust in her, to hack her computer, and yours. Then you discovered everything.

"I was so scared Dermot and Daniel would be the ones who'd be dragged into this when everything they'd done came to light during the investigation. I found only one way out. To tell you it was Glory."

And he groaned with six years of heartache. "*Per Dio,* why? Didn't you think what you'd be doing to her, to me? Didn't you realize how much I loved her?"

"It was because I knew exactly how much you loved her that I did this. I knew you loved her so much you might forgive her, or at least wouldn't be able to bring yourself to punish her, would let her get away with it—let us—let *me*—get away with it. And I was right. You did."

He shook his head in disbelief. "You don't consider breaking her heart a punishment?"

"It was her heart or my husband's and son's lives."

Silence crushed down as he gazed into the woman's drowned eyes, the pieces falling into place like hammers.

Then he said, "Then it happened again."

Her tears ran continuously now. "They gave me the new assignment as soon as your wedding was announced. I begged them to let me go, tried to tell them that there was no way you wouldn't be prepared this time, that you wouldn't find out. They only said that with Glory as your wife now, it would be impossible to guard yourself, and that even if you found out, you wouldn't be able to expose her—or rather me. They didn't care what happened as long as they got their info. I owed them for giving them what had turned out to be useless info before. And they still owned my men. So I did it again. But I was only waiting until you caught me at it."

"But you still left tracks leading to Glory, to take refuge in my love for her again."

Her face crumbled. "And I was right again. Even when you thought she'd betrayed you twice, you wouldn't have ever hurt her."

His groan was agonized. "I already hurt her beyond what you can imagine. I'm only now beginning to realize the magnitude of the pain and damage I caused her."

She clung to his arm, her feeble grip barely registering. "I beg you, don't blame yourself. It was all my doing."

He covered her hand with his. "I do and will blame myself. I loved her, should have given her the benefit of the doubt. I didn't. And I hurt her so much she no longer wants to have anything to do with me."

"No, Vincenzo. You're her heart. She must only be running away to lick her wounds. She's shocked and anguished at what I did. Don't give up on her, I beg you."

He hugged her gently, defusing her panic. "I would give up on life before I gave up on Glory." He withdrew to wipe the tears of the woman he now hoped would live to see his and Glory's children and be their grandmother for long years to come.

"Now give me names. I'll get those people who've turned your lives into a living hell off your backs once and for all."

Keeping his promise to Glenda had taken far longer than he could stand. Two full, unending days.

But at least it was over. He'd terminated the hold those mob bosses had over the Monaghans' lives.

Contrary to Glenda's belief, he wasn't so refined that he couldn't handle criminal scum. He'd negotiated a perfect deal with them. He'd paid more than handsomely for the lost revenue ensuing from losing some of their efficient operatives. And he'd let them know how much they'd lose, in every way, if they came after his and Glory's family, or his work, ever again.

Now one thing remained. The only thing that mattered to him anymore in the world. Glory.

"We'll get to her in time, *Principe*."

Vincenzo gritted his teeth at Alonzo's assurance. He didn't know if they would. The flight taking her away to Darfur was in less than an hour. She must already be at the gate. Not that he'd let that stop him. Even if she flew away, he'd follow her. To the ends of the earth.

In minutes that passed like torturous hours, Alonzo pulled up at the airport's departure zone. He lowered the window as Vincenzo exploded from the car, yelling after him, "Just ring when you get your princess back, *Principe*. I'll be waiting to drive you back home."

Vincenzo ran, Alonzo's last words skewering his heart.

If he didn't get her back, he'd never go home. He had no home to go to without her.

But then, not getting her back wasn't an option.

He tore across the airport, only stopping to ask about Glory's flight. It was boarding in twenty minutes.

He bought a ticket, produced his diplomatic passport and begged for security checks to be rushed so he could catch up with his runaway bride. Then he was streaking across the airport, bumping into people left and right. He'd run out of sorrys by the time he'd reached her gate.

She was standing in line, holding her boarding pass and

one of those nondescript handbags of hers, looking terrible. And the most wonderful sight he'd ever seen. The only one he wanted to live his life seeing.

His heart kicked his ribs so hard it had him stumbling into another run, pushing through the line to reach her. She was so deep in her misery she only noticed the commotion he'd caused when someone bumped into her. Her eyes, his own pieces of heaven, looked up at him with a world of pain and desperation.

The drain of anxiety and the surge of relief shook his arms as he enfolded her and his voice as he groaned against her cheek, her neck, her lips, "Come home with me, *amore,* I beg you."

She only went inert in his embrace.

Deadness crept up Glory's body like fast-growing vines.

She welcomed its suffocation, its stability, which allowed her to stand in the circle of his arms, feeling his beloved body seeking her and enfolding her, without collapsing in a mass of misery.

It also gave her the strength to push away, even though she felt she pushed away from her life source.

She staggered a step, barely aware of the hundreds of people around, watching them. She had eyes and senses only for Vincenzo, for noticing how his hair and face were captured by the atrocious lighting of the airport, enhancing every gleam, emphasizing every jut and hollow.

A blaze of love and longing shriveled her heart. She'd been too optimistic thinking there had been a chance she'd survive this. There wasn't.

He reached for her again, hands urgent, coaxing, moving over her back, her arms, her face, leaving each feeling forever scarred with the memory of what she'd never have again.

"Come with me, *amore,*" he urged again.

"I can't." Her voice sounded as dead as she felt.

"You can't do anything else, *amore*. You belong with me. To me. You're the only one for me."

"That's not true, never was, never will be."

His arms fell away, and he looked at her as if she'd just emptied a gun in his gut.

"You—you don't…" His bit his lower lip then his voice plunged to a hoarse rasp that sounded like pain and dread made audible. "You don't love me?"

She should say she didn't. He'd stop blaming himself for his role in her devastation, stop trying to make amends. This was what he was here doing, after all. And she no longer blamed him for anything. She only wanted to set him free.

She still couldn't bring herself to lie. Not about this.

She escaped answering. "I am not the one for you, Vincenzo. *Anyone* else would be better for you. Anyone who doesn't have a family with a criminal history."

His devastated expression fell apart with the snap of tension, morphed into the very sight of relief. "This is what you meant? What you're thinking?"

"It's not what I'm thinking. It's the truth."

"According to whom?"

"To the world."

"Does it look like I care what the world does or doesn't think?"

He spread his arms, encompassing the scene around them. Everyone was staring openly at them, the buzz of recognition, curiosity and amusement rising. Some were even taking photos and recording videos.

Embarrassment crept up her face. "You do care or you wouldn't have married me as a social facade. And when the truth comes out…"

"It never will."

"…it will cost you and Castaldini too much. That's why

it's a fact that any woman who doesn't have a family with a criminal history and connections would be better for you."

"No one is better for me. No one is better, period." She started to shake her head, her heart ricocheting inside her rib cage at his intensity and the unwilling rise of hope. He caught her face, his hands gentleness and persuasion itself. "And pretending to care about that social facade was just so I could have you without admitting the truth. All those years I've been looking for a way to have you again. Because I haven't been truly alive since I walked away from you. And now I can't live without you. I only cared about your family's crimes when I thought you'd been involved in them, but lately, not even then. And now none of that is an issue. I've managed to wipe your family's slate clean."

"Y-you did…? How?"

He told her, quickly, urgently, as if needing to get this out of the way, to move on to what he considered relevant.

And she felt her world disintegrating around her again.

"I never suspected… I always thought… God!" Tears gushed, then burned down her cheeks. "The years I spent being angry at Dad and Daniel, thinking they were irresponsible, criminal, when they…they…"

He dragged her to him, protecting her from her anguish, all the missing parts of her fitting back. "You can now have your family back, forgive them for everything that has been beyond them and be happy loving them again."

She raised her eyes to his, unable to grasp the enormity of it all. "How can you be so…so forgiving, so generous, after all they've done to you?"

"Conceiving you is an achievement that would make up for any past or future crime. And then they were under threat. A threat I ended, so they can now go on with their lives without the shadow of fear."

She started to protest and he scooped her up in his arms,

clamping his lips over hers. As the power of his kiss dragged her down into a well of craving, she thought she heard hoots of approval and clapping.

He pulled away, groaning, "*Gloria mia, ti voglio, ti amo*— I'm going crazy wanting you, loving you."

She felt he was letting her look deep into his soul, letting her see what she'd always thought would remain an impossible fantasy. Vincenzo didn't only love her, his love was as fierce and total as hers.

But this was why she'd had to walk away. So she wouldn't disrupt his life and destiny.

She had to protect him, especially since he clearly wasn't willing to protect himself. "You can't only consider your heart…you have duties, a status, and I'm…"

He clamped his lips on hers again, aborting her panting protest. "My first duty is to you. My status depends on honoring you first."

She shook her head. "My family…if the truth comes out… God, Vincenzo, you can't have them for your in-laws…."

His expression was resoluteness itself. "I already have them as my in-laws, and they'll always be my in-laws, and I will be proud to have them as the family of our children."

"Our ch-childr…" With those two magical words, a fierce yearning sheared through her, draining every spark of tension holding her together. She swooned in his hold.

His arms tightened until she felt he was trying to merge them. "Yes, our children, as many and as soon as you want."

The magnitude of what he was offering, the future he was painting, stunned her into silence as her mind's eye tremblingly tried to imagine it all. A future, a whole life, filled with love and alliance and trust, with him. Children with him. Even her family back, because of him.

Vincenzo took advantage of her silence and strode away with her still in his arms, talking to many people, then on the phone. She watched everything from the security of his embrace, as if from the depths of a dream. Somewhere it registered that he was arranging their exit after they'd been checked in as far as the boarding gate and arranging for her luggage to be sent back.

Then a sound penetrated the fog of her bliss. A horn.

Her dazed gaze panned around, found Vincenzo's car with Alonzo at the wheel, waving to them urgently as he stopped in an unloading-only zone.

In seconds, Vincenzo had her inside the cool, dim seclusion of the limo. As Alonzo maneuvered smoothly into the traffic, Vincenzo bundled her onto his lap.

After a kiss that left her breathless, he drew away, his faced gripped in the passion she couldn't wait to have him expend all over her.

"I have to get this out of the way once and forever, *gloriosa mia,* then we'll never speak or think of it again. You had nothing to do with your family's mistakes. You are the one woman I could ever love, the soul mate I would be forever proud to call mine, and to call myself yours. I truly care nothing about what the world will bring me as long as you're mine forever."

Her head rolled over his shoulder, her lids and insides heavy with need. Every nerve alight with delight at his declarations, she caressed the wonder of his hard cheek. "As long as you understand it will probably take the rest of my life to get used to all those unbelievable facts."

He pressed another urgent, devouring kiss on her lips as if compelled to do it. "I don't think there is any such thing as 'getting used' to this—" he hugged her tighter "—what we share. Just to always marvel at it, be humbled by it and thankful for it."

Then his smile suddenly dissolved, leaving his face a mask of gravity. Her heart quivered with a tremor of uncertainty.

Then, with all the solemnity of a pledge, he said, "Will you marry me again, Glory? This time with our love declared, because we are each other's destiny?"

Joy exploded inside her, making her erupt in his arms and rain tears and kisses all over his beloved face and hands. "Yes, Vincenzo. Yes, yes, *yes,* to everything, forever."

Smiling elatedly, as choked with emotion as she, his own eyes filling with tears, Vincenzo took her lips, drowning her in the miracle of his love.

Deep from the security of his love and embrace she heard Alonzo exclaiming, "*Eccellente.* I not only get my princess back, I get to arrange another wedding. But now with true love declared and the catastrophe of separation averted, this calls for a much more elaborate ceremony."

Glory gaped up at Vincenzo. "There could be anything more elaborate?"

Vincenzo poured indulgence over her, pinching her buttock playfully. "Have you even met Alonzo?"

Carefree giggles burst out of her for the first time in... She didn't even remember when she'd laughed so freely.

But she still had to make a stand. "While I loved the first ceremony, Alonzo, I really would rather we used all the expenses in something...uh..."

Alonzo smirked at her in the rearview mirror. "Is *worthwhile* the word you're looking for?" At her apologetic nod, he sighed. "I can see it's not going to be as much fun as I thought having a philanthropist for a princess."

At her chuckling sigh, Vincenzo smoothed the hair he'd mussed off her face lovingly. "How about we have everything? The figure you name for your worthwhile endeavors, the all-out-expenses wedding—" He turned to meet Alonzo's eyes in the mirror. "Preferably a double wedding this time."

She looked between both men then exclaimed, "Gio proposed?"

A smile of pure happiness spread Alonzo's lips, even as his green eyes misted. "Ah, *si*…and how he did."

She waited until he stopped at a traffic light, then exploded from Vincenzo's arms and jumped on Alonzo, hugging him and soundly kissing him on his widely smiling cheek.

After she milked him for details and whooped and exclaimed with excitement over being his matron of honor, he resumed driving.

She returned to the place she never wanted to leave, burrowed deep in Vincenzo's embrace, letting the last of her tension escape in a long sigh.

Stroking her hair gently, Vincenzo echoed her sigh, the sound of contentment. "Take us home, Alonzo."

Many, many hours later, a delightfully sore and thoroughly sated Glory turned luxuriantly in her lover, prince and husband's arms, filling her eyes with his beauty. "Is it possible? Could everything be so perfect?"

He shifted to accommodate her closer, sweeping caresses down her back and buttocks, as if imprinting his love into her, coating her with satisfaction. "If you need some imperfections to settle your mind, I have plenty for you. Like having to start my negotiations from scratch and roping you in as my top consultant. Like trying to create a method so I can get hands-on, steady involvements in your missions."

Her eyes widened with each word. "God, Vincenzo…you mean it?" At his smiling nod, she tackled him on his back and attacked him with kisses and tickles. He was guffawing by the time she pulled back, frowning. "But wait—that's only more perfection." She threw herself beside him on her back, covered her eyes and cried out, "Argh, I can't stand it."

He rose above her, letting her fill her soul with his unbridled love. Then he suddenly cupped her breast, lazily flicked her nipple, a look of mischief replacing the passion. "You can't? Shall I leave you to rest then?"

She pulled him on top of her. "Don't you *dare*."

As she took him inside her again, as he joined them into one flesh, one future, she thanked the fates that nothing, not betrayal nor pain, not desperation nor separation, had dimmed this miracle they had between them.

And now she knew. Nothing ever would.

* * * *

Don't miss CONVENIENTLY HIS PRINCESS,
the next novel in the
MARRIED BY ROYAL DECREE *series.*
Travel back to the exotic desert kingdom of Zohayd, where
a man searching for a home must take a
princess as his convenient bride. Or so he thinks.
Available September 2013!
Only from Olivia Gates and Harlequin Desire.

#2233 SUNSET SEDUCTION
The Slades of Sunset Ranch
Charlene Sands
When the chance to jump into bed with longtime crush Lucas Slade comes along, Audrey Thomas can't help but seize it. Now the tricky part is to wrangle her way into the rich rancher's *heart*.

#2234 AFFAIRS OF STATE
Daughters of Power: The Capital
Jennifer Lewis
Can Ariella Winthrop—revealed as the secret love child of the U.S. president—find love with a royal prince whose family disapproves of her illegitimacy?

#2235 HIS FOR THE TAKING
Rich, Rugged Ranchers
Ann Major
It's been six years since Maddie Gray left town in disgrace. But now she's back, and wealthy rancher John Coleman can't stay away from the lover who once betrayed him.

#2236 TAMING THE LONE WOLFF
The Men of Wolff Mountain
Janice Maynard
Security expert Larkin Wolff lives by a code, but when he's hired to protect an innocent heiress, he's tempted to break all his rules and become *personally* involved with his client....

#2237 HOLLYWOOD HOUSE CALL
Jules Bennett
When an accident forces receptionist Callie Matthews to move in with her boss, her relationship with the sexy doctor becomes much less about business and *very* much about pleasure....

#2238 THE FIANCÉE CHARADE
The Pearl House
Fiona Brand
Faced with losing custody of her daughter, Gemma O'Neill will do anything—even pretend to be engaged to the man who fathered her child.

HDCNM0513

REQUEST YOUR FREE BOOKS!
2 FREE NOVELS PLUS 2 FREE GIFTS!

♦HARLEQUIN®

Desire

ALWAYS POWERFUL, PASSIONATE AND PROVOCATIVE

YES! Please send me 2 FREE Harlequin Desire® novels and my 2 FREE gifts (gifts are worth about $10). After receiving them, if I don't wish to receive any more books, I can return the shipping statement marked "cancel." If I don't cancel, I will receive 6 brand-new novels every month and be billed just $4.55 per book in the U.S. or $4.99 per book in Canada. That's a savings of at least 13% off the cover price! It's quite a bargain! Shipping and handling is just 50¢ per book in the U.S. and 75¢ per book in Canada.* I understand that accepting the 2 free books and gifts places me under no obligation to buy anything. I can always return a shipment and cancel at any time. Even if I never buy another book, the two free books and gifts are mine to keep forever.

225/326 HDN F4ZC

Name	(PLEASE PRINT)
Address	Apt. #
City	State/Prov.	Zip/Postal Code

Signature (if under 18, a parent or guardian must sign)

Mail to the Harlequin® Reader Service:

IN U.S.A.: P.O. Box 1867, Buffalo, NY 14240-1867
IN CANADA: P.O. Box 609, Fort Erie, Ontario L2A 5X3

Want to try two free books from another line?
Call 1-800-873-8635 or visit www.ReaderService.com.

* Terms and prices subject to change without notice. Prices do not include applicable taxes. Sales tax applicable in N.Y. Canadian residents will be charged applicable taxes. Offer not valid in Quebec. This offer is limited to one order per household. Not valid for current subscribers to Harlequin Desire books. All orders subject to credit approval. Credit or debit balances in a customer's account(s) may be offset by any other outstanding balance owed by or to the customer. Please allow 4 to 6 weeks for delivery. Offer available while quantities last.

Your Privacy—The Harlequin® Reader Service is committed to protecting your privacy. Our Privacy Policy is available online at www.ReaderService.com or upon request from the Harlequin Reader Service.

We make a portion of our mailing list available to reputable third parties that offer products we believe may interest you. If you prefer that we not exchange your name with third parties, or if you wish to clarify or modify your communication preferences, please visit us at www.ReaderService.com/consumerschoice or write to us at Harlequin Reader Service Preference Service, P.O. Box 9062, Buffalo, NY 14269. Include your complete name and address.

HDI3R

SPECIAL EXCERPT FROM

presents

SUNSET SEDUCTION

The latest installment of USA TODAY *bestselling author*

Charlene Sands's miniseries

THE SLADES OF SUNSET RANCH

All grown up, Audrey Faith Thomas seizes her chance to act on a teenage crush. Now she must face the consequences....

Usually not much unnerved Audrey Faith Thomas, except for the time when her big brother was bucked off Old Stormy at an Amarillo rodeo and broke his back.

Audrey shuddered at the memory and thanked the Almighty that Casey was alive and well and bossy as ever. But as she sat behind the wheel of her car, driving toward her fate, the fear coursing through her veins had nothing to do with her brother's disastrous five-second ride. This fear was much different. It made her want to turn her Chevy pickup truck around and go home to Reno and forget all about showing up at Sunset Ranch unannounced.

To face Lucas Slade.

The man she'd seduced and then abandoned in the middle of the night.

Audrey swallowed hard. She still couldn't believe what she'd done.

Last month, after an argument and a three week standoff with her brother, she'd ventured to his Lake Tahoe cabin to